This book is dedicated to my friend Graeme Brady of Nelson, New Zealand. Graeme died of cancer in 2020. He suggested that I write a book that would bring death to life, and during the months before he passed away, he sent me regular emails telling me what it was like to die happily.

Some of the characters, scenes and thoughts in this book derive from his creative mind, but he cannot be held responsible for the vagaries of my mind.

Graeme died magnificently. It will not surprise you that the dominant character in this book is named Graeme.

A Beautiful Sunset

A novel about the final curtain call of life

Everald Compton

ECHO BOOKS

First Published in 2021 by Echo Books

Echo Books is an imprint of Superscript Publishing Pty Ltd, ABN 76 644 812 395

Registered Office: Suite 401, 140 Bourke St, Melbourne, VIC, 3000

www.echobooks.com.au

Copyright ©Everald Compton

Creator: Compton, Everald: Author

Title: A Beautiful Sunset: A novel about the final curtain call of life

ISBN: 978-0-6488546-0-9 (soft cover)

A catalogue record for this book is available from the National Library of Australia

Book layout and design by Peter Gamble, Canberra

Set in Garamond Premier Pro Display, 12/17 and Bon Vivant Serif

Also by Everald Compton

The Man on the Twenty Dollar Notes [published by Xlibris in 2016]
Dinner with the Founding Fathers [published by Austin Macauley in 2020].

Contents

Foreword

This book honours the memory of a British Army officer, Captain Lawrence Oates. He died at Ross Shelf in Antarctica on 17 May 1912. Oates was a member of a British expedition, led by Captain Robert Falcon Scott. They were attempting to achieve the honour of being the first humans to reach the South Pole.

They did reach the Pole, but only to find that Roald Amundsen of Norway had reached it several weeks earlier, leaving behind a Norwegian flag to mark his achievement. On their lonely and disheartened journey back to their boat, Scott's expedition experienced abnormally freezing weather, wild winds and huge snowdrifts. Many were injured by falls and suffered severe scurvy and frostbite.

When they were just twenty kilometres from the boat, Oates found that he could walk no further, and, knowing that his team members could not carry him, he decided to end his life. That evening, Oates lay huddled in a tent with his friends. Painfully dragging himself to his feet, he raised the flap of the tent and said to Scott, 'I am just going outside and may be some time.' The team tried to restrain him, but they did not have the strength.

Oates lies permanently frozen under the polar icecap. He died by voluntary euthanasia. No historian, nor British Army records, describe his passing as suicide, and they never will. He is revered to this day as a national hero of Britain.

When Scott's diary was found, these words were recorded in it on the night of his colleague's death: 'Oates was a very gallant gentleman.'

Author's Notes

I have based this novel on the lives of four human beings who face death, as well as their doctor who becomes personally involved in their struggle and who comes to terms with the relationship of birth, life and death in their final days.

I do not identify the city where these characters live, nor the nation in which this story is located, as it could happen anywhere in the world. This is a tale of people, not places. But you can be assured that it is a nation that has laws approving of voluntary assisted dying (VAD). I also don't go into details about the medical issues surrounding their deaths, as I am not qualified to comment on the science of medicine. I simply convey the fact that they are dying from commonly known causes.

The first of the interesting characters is a Christian of radical theology who is a famous and best selling author. He has terminal cancer and chooses an early death via VAD, thus incurring the wrath of conservative church leaders.

The second character is the exact opposite: an ultra-fundamentalist Christian in both faith and politics, as well as a passionate advocate of the Prosperity Gospel. He is certain that he is one of God's chosen people and therefore immune to Covid-19, a belief that proves fatal.

The third is an atheist who has mental health issues and rejects spiritual solutions to them. This leads her to believe that suicide is her only option, and she acts on it.

The fourth is a one-hundred-year-old man who has led a successful life and who is in full possession of his mental faculties, but his old body is losing its life and just hanging together. He simply wants to end it for personal reasons, and he plans decisive action to die by VAD in Switzerland.

All four characters share the same doctor, a Muslim woman rejected by those of her own religion because she refuses to accepts the male domination of her life and faith, and their belief that only Allah can decide who lives and dies.

A mentor to them all is a little old lady, the local Miss Marple who quietly gets around helping people solve their problems. She is a person of little education, simple habits and meagre finances. Her life has always been a huge struggle, but she has survived by following a religion called 'common sense', which she believes is the most powerful expression of faith that it is possible to find.

I have added to the mix is a Jewish rabbi, a dedicated Buddhist, an Anglican bishop and an interesting Confucian, as well as an eminent lawyer and an aggressive widow, all of whom bring differing views of death to the scene. There is also a media personality who decides to crusade against VAD.

In telling their compelling story in challenging terms, I hope that readers will engage with me in robust debate that will help us all to happily and positively comprehend the reality of death.

Right now, I am at the end of my ninth decade and look forward to a productive tenth leading me to a happy departure. Whatever age my readers are, I hope that this book will ensure that none of us will ever fear death, but will instead enjoy a beautiful sunset.

Everald Compton
Brisbane
February 2021

Chapter One

'Mr Brown. It is with great sadness that I tell you that you have no more than three months to live.'

Dr Aisha Jinnah, a gentle soul, looked at her patient with compassion. She had spoken bluntly and clearly as she intended to be absolutely sure that he fully understood the stark reality of her comments and his fate.

Graeme Brown remained silent for quite a while, staring at his Muslim doctor in bewilderment. Then he stared blankly at the wall, as if words would somehow appear there saying this is all just nonsense. He tried to speak, stammering a bit as he struggled to put his thoughts into words.

'I am fully aware of the turmoil that has just seized your mental processes, Mr Brown.'

Aisha's words broke his trance.

'You are asking yourself,' she continued, 'why it is that, after a year of using every type of cancer therapy that had the capacity to cure you, and after which there were such promising initial results, you now receive this unexpected knockout blow.'

'I would not describe it as a knockout blow, but I am certainly down for a long count. To put it mildly, I'm debating whether I want to get up off the mat at this moment. What has caused our initial hopes to be so badly misguided?'

'Let me put it simply. We treated your primary bowel cancer far too late. We managed to retard its growth for a while, and we believed that we could create conditions in which you could live with your cancer. Sadly, we could not stop its inevitable advance. Its cells have quietly spread to five other parts of your body, and suddenly they are very aggressive. It's now unstoppable. There are too many bad cells floating around your body in every direction. I had considerable difficulty believing it myself as it revealed itself so quickly, so I sought independent opinions from several eminent cancer experts who were not part of the experienced team you and I have been working with. They fully endorsed our final assessment of your condition. I have their opinions and ours in an envelope for you to read at home. If you wish, I can also arrange for you to meet them as a matter of urgency.'

'Well, I guess this is life. It is what it is. I don't want to waste any time checking up on your diagnosis.'

'Death is part of life, Mr Brown. It is an experience that every one of us is certain to encounter sooner or later. You will handle it better than most, because my assessment of your personality over several years is that you will decide that the best way to handle this is to enjoy your final days.'

'It certainly is the grand finale of my life, and I am thinking that I must do far more than enjoy it. The smart thing to do is welcome it with open arms and at least have a spiritual victory over it. I can recall preaching a sermon a decade ago in which I said that people who are afraid of death are also afraid of life. To avoid being a hypocrite, I must now live and die without fear.'

'I am hugely impressed by your attitude, Mr Brown. It will make your final pathway much easier for you to tread, and for your family and friends too.'

'My prime concern at this moment is to work out how I should go about conveying this news to them in a way that will cause minimum shock and pain.'

'Perhaps you should use the same words that I did when I opened this conversation.'

'They were blunt.'

'But they laid the basis for a responsible discussion about life and death. Nothing would have been achieved had I played games with words.'

'True.'

'Can I be of some help to you by inviting your family to meet me so I can answer all their questions about your medical condition?'

'Thank you, but no. It's important that I handle this personally. The bonds that unite my family are strong, but this news will shake us to the core. I think they will want to chat about my mental and spiritual capacity to handle this shock, rather than concern themselves about why I am dying.'

'Okay. May I now comment on the options for pain relief in these final days? I feel confident that we can keep you out of pain without reducing your brain power or stopping you from being mobile. Towards the end, you may need a battery-powered wheelchair.'

'Thank you, again, but can we leave it for this moment. I know that I will need relief from pain, but it will be for just a short time as I intend to end of life by using voluntary assisted dying. I will be grateful if you will be the doctor who will lead me through all the medical and legal certifications that will be needed.'

'You and I have discussed this on several occasions during this past year of treatment as your clear intent if it all turned out badly. I know that this is your rational choice. So, my answer is yes, and I will ensure that you have the best palliative care that is available while the legal requirements of voluntary assisted dying are completed.'

'I greatly appreciate the huge effort you have made over these last difficult months of intensive treatment to save my life. I am confident that you will help me on my pathway to death after having enjoyed life so much.'

'Go now with peace in your heart as you meet your family,' said Dr Jinnah. 'May you join together as a united team to come to terms with this once-in-a-lifetime crisis.'

'I will, but it will require a significant effort at this moment for me to achieve peace in my soul and to help them do likewise.'

With a smile and a wave, Graeme headed for the door. But then he paused and turned around. With hesitance, he moved towards Aisha.

'I know that I am transgressing Muslim religion, culture and tradition, but may I give you a well-meaning hug?'

'May I reverse your wish to show thanks? Let me give you a hug. It will preserve Muslim dignity if I claim that it was part of the medical treatment I am obliged as a good doctor to give you for the preservation of your soul.'

The hug lasted longer than medical protocol required, and it gave impetus to Graeme's first step onto the stage for his final curtain call. Without another word, a dying man in the sixtieth year of his life left to face his destiny.

As he paid the bill on the way out, the receptionist pointed out to him that his credit card was about to expire. His response was quite pleasantly pragmatic.

'I don't think I will bother to renew it when they send me a reminder. I have a few other cards. Most have a few months left and for me this is a lifetime.'

They both smiled. There really was no alternative.

———

'Mr Palmer, you have tested positive for Covid-19.'

The soft voice of Dr Aisha Jinnah came down the phone like a thunderclap that shook the recipient from stem to stern. Scott Palmer was disbelieving. Indeed, he was offended by such a blatant untruth. This nonsense was not in God's grand plan for his life.

'This cannot possibly be correct, Doctor.'

'Why can't it be, Mr Palmer? I have the pathologists report on my computer right now showing the results of your Covid-19 test as being positive. It quite clearly shows your name. I will email it to you as we speak.'

'Please do that so I can keep it as a souvenir, but I am certain that it is an administrative error based on information that clearly belongs to someone else. God protects those who sincerely believe in Him. I am committed to Him heart and soul. Totally. He will not betray me.'

'Mr Palmer, I respect your deep Christian commitment, but I have to act upon the professional medical report in front of me. To affirm my respect for you, and to ensure that this report is not in error, I will arrange for another test to be done today by another experienced pathologist. But while we wait for it, you must immediately remain in total isolation at home.'

'Why can't we delay any isolation until we get proof that this is a fake report?'

'Not possible. My initial diagnosis was that you had severe influenza and should isolate at home. You took no notice of me and went about your normal routine. You thought you just had a bad cold. May I respectfully suggest that you act responsibly while we prove whether your doubts are right or wrong?'

'Please do so quickly as this is all absolute humbug. My God has an important purpose for me in life and coronavirus is not part of His plans for me.'

'I will move quickly. One of my nurses will come to your home within the hour to take a swab. As I have indicated, she will deliver it immediately to a different pathologist than the one who handled the first test, asking for it to be processed urgently today. You are aware that you will have significant fees to pay for this special service? I presume that this will cause you no concern.'

'Thank you. Tell the pathologist I will pay triple their normal fees to get an answer by tonight.'

Scott cut off the call without a parting greeting. This intrusion had been the work of idiots. His discourtesy did not cause Aisha any concern whatsoever. She knew that he rarely, if ever, said goodbye. His sense of a higher calling meant that he recognised no need to be involved in the social trivialities that concerned lesser beings.

Aisha pondered the difference evident in the lives and personalities of Scott Palmer and Graeme Brown. When she had delivered even worse news about life and death to Graeme a few days ago, his reaction had been starkly different.

She called in her next patient, hoping that this person had some vestige of humility.

———

Meanwhile, back at the Palmer home, Pauline, Scott's wife, called out to ask Scott what was going on in his life. She was a rigidly fundamentalist Christian, whereas her husband was a high-powered, happy-clappy Pentecostal.

'Nothing at all. I will have some new pathology results by tonight that will sensibly determine what ails me. There are no worries at present, and I am cancelling my appointments for the rest of the day.'

He took his laptop with him as he walked to a comfortable chair where he could peacefully carry out God's work. Despite a strange lack of energy that baffled and worried him, he had vital work to do. Coughing regularly and somewhat painfully, he set about furthering the successful business ventures to which God had called him, and which were powered by the Prosperity Gospel, the world's least-used spiritual and economic fire power.

———

Julia Hawke had made a chilling decision. Her life would end. Right now. This very night. She could think of no valid reason to remain alive for one day longer.

Her daughter, Sarah, had left her some time ago, declaring that she despised her and that their alienation from one another was permanent and irreversible. Julia was unemployed and dead broke, with ever mounting debts, especially for the rent on her home.

Julia should not have been in this position. She was a qualified law clerk, but she lacked the personal skills required to be competent at legal work in cooperation with others. The problem appeared to be that most of her potential employers seemed to instinctively sense that she was a possible problem, as her capacity to sustain personal relationships was fragile and, far too often, volatile. Nevertheless, her career could have been revived.

Compounding her problems was her snap decision to totally give up her belief in God. Her incomplete understanding of God was something instilled by her father, created in her mind by fear and by repeatedly telling her that his sexual abuse of her was God's will.

She now considered herself to be a long-term atheist, and because of that conviction she found life to be utterly meaningless, a state of mind that most atheists certainly would not share. She knew that when she took her life, there would be no reprisals by any god. If there was a place called Hell, it could be no worse that the environment in which she 'lived' right now. There was every possibility that it may be better.

Her mobile phone was in her hand. It was her only permanent and genuine companion. Without it she had no sense of security or confidence in herself. But soon she would be no longer able to pay the monthly rental. In preparation for the end of her life, she calmly and deliberately sent a text to the only person whom she considered to be a real friend. She desperately needed assurance that someone would care that she was gone. Dr Aisha Jinnah. Aisha would understand and would not be shocked. She had gone through her own experience of personal hell in the land of her birth, and had now reached the eminent position as a leader of community health.

Quietly and purposefully, as she sat on a lonely and cold park bench, she tapped away on her phone to send Aisha a text message: 'Thank you, Aisha. You have reached out to me in a loving manner that no one before has ever tried to do. I have done nothing to either earn or deserve your friendship, but it has kept me going through dark days. Now it all has no purpose and must end tonight. May you continue the good work of compassion that you freely give to people like me.'

Removing a sharp steak knife from her handbag, she hesitatingly slashed away at her wrists, with fear in her heart, and watched in a trance as her life blood started to flow. She sensed her world slowly beginning to fade away as she threw herself on to the ground, sobbing her heart away.

———

Aisha was near her phone when it beeped. Instantly, she assessed that this was not an idle thought in a troubled mind. She phoned Julia. No answer. Sent a text. No response.

Aisha ran to her car and headed for Julia's modest home. It was just five minutes away in a quiet street where parking was easy. She swung into Julia's driveway and jumped out quickly. The lights of her decaying home were off, and all of the doors were locked.

She phoned again. No answer once more. Another text. Same result. Exercising her only practical option, she phoned the emergency services and requested police and an ambulance to come urgently. They arrived within ten minutes. Aisha explained that she was a doctor and that the occupant of this house had texted her to say she was ending her life. The police forced entry into the house, but it was empty.

Aisha was at a loss for words. She asked the police if they would be willing to issue a general alert for a woman whose life was in danger. She gave them a clear description of Julia.

Thankfully, they agreed and acted immediately. Then Aisha remembered she had a photo of Julia in her phone and she sent it to them.

The police officer had a comment. 'Last night I was called to a car accident. It had hit a post on an overhead bridge at high speed. Only the driver was in it. Very dead. No other cars around. Bystanders said it looked like a deliberate hit. There was nothing obvious that could have caused the accident. Today the family confirmed that the guy had terminal cancer. It was a clear case of voluntary euthanasia carried out in the crudest possible way, but opponents to euthanasia persistently ignore it. My fellow officers tell me that it happens often. Does your patient have a terminal illness?'

'No, but she has severe mental-health issues.'

'Well, this means that we have no option but to take this very seriously. Bye for now.'

Aisha quickly returned to her car and sat quietly as she pondered all the possibilities. There were not many, but the police's theory was worth following up. She then realised that Julia could not have been in a car accident. Her car had been confiscated by the leasing company for regular defaults on payments over a long period of time. Maybe she could have thrown herself in front of a car? But she doubted it.

She drove home feeling greatly frustrated that she had no option but to wait for the police to tell her whether Julia was alive or dead.

Jamie Glasgow was celebrating birthday number one hundred. He 'lived' in aged care at a place called 'The Haven', which was anything but that. It was owned and managed by a large commercial company of property developers, who ran it as a maximum-profit venture with little recognition that their residents were human beings. They did likewise with fifty other aged-care centres in an empire across the nation.

Jamie was making a brief speech to the one hundred fellow residents of The Haven who were all seated in the lounge where they had enjoyed a slice of delicious birthday cake provided by Jamie's daughter-in-law, Annie, who had cooked it herself.

Jamie was seated as his old legs were not as active as they used to be, and his arthritis was bad and getting worse. There was evidence also that Parkinson's was setting in. But his speech, just like his heart, was clear and strong.

'Thank you for honouring me today on my one hundredth birthday,' he said. 'It is very kind of you all and I am grateful. May I especially thank Annie for making the cake. She is a wonderful cook, which is why I have lived so long. I am delighted also that my doctor, Aisha Jinnah, is here. She is a prime reason why I have had a long life, as she is immensely talented and a loving soul. But there is really only one reason why I have lived for a century.

God put me into the world so that I could use the talents he gave me to create a better world, and I have spent my life doing my best to achieve just that. May God bless you all.'

Aisha came over to greet him. 'Good speech, Jamie, and warm congratulations on living for a hundred years.'

'Thank you, Aisha. For so many years you have gone overboard in your great efforts to give me a good life. You are a beautiful person.'

'Jamie, you have been a lovely patient to deal with. Now, can you tell me what your plans are for the coming year?'

'I want to die.'

Chapter Two

As one of the few female doctors of Arabian descent and Islamic faith in her new homeland, Aisha Jinnah was fortunate to be alive, let alone prospering and in a position of professional responsibility. In her early years in the Middle East, she had been raped and beaten and starved and humiliated, but she had risen above it all through sheer will power.

Now she was a respected general practitioner skilled in handling patients in crisis situations. She was in a sound position to give focused care to Graeme, Scott, Julia and Jamie who were facing the greatest challenges of their lives.

A couple of decades ago, Aisha had escaped from her homeland by an absolute stroke of good fortune that enabled her to cross two borders. She made it safely through by negotiating an extraordinary political fluke in the harsh system that controls the borders of her new homeland. She now treasured it as a place that offered enormous possibilities for aspirational people.

As a youth in her homeland, she had received a limited education, learning only to read the Koran while preparing herself to be a loyal wife and mother for the rest of her days, though she fought this fate. When she established herself in a new life, she enjoyed its wonderful world of education. She was quite simply amazed at the wide range of opportunities available to women willing to be part of a progressively brave team, and who were now breaking the glass ceiling of prejudice and discrimination in so many exciting ways.

Aisha took full advantage of the new privileges she now cherished and eventually graduated as a Doctor of Medicine.

She was now utterly devoted to her work and had never married. Indeed, she gave it sparse consideration. Her opinion of men was very low, given the atrocities she experienced as a youth. The thought of a sexual relationship with even the gentlest and kindest of men was repulsive. But in its place, she had developed an acute sense of humanity, a great love of people and an ability to accept verbal abuse without getting upset about it. She lived in hope that physical abuse was now an element of life that was unlikely to trouble her again.

It would be more than fair to say that Aisha wanted to love everyone in a way that combined emotion with wisdom, and she only retreated from that intent when someone outrightly rejected her as a person. Even then, she did not loathe or hate anyone who stood in her path and demeaned her. They simply became of little consequence on the road of life.

She did, however, have a male friend who had come recently into her life. He was a follower of Confucius, and his homeland was the Chinese island of Hainan. His name was Mencius, a revered name among Confucians as Mencius was a philosopher who took the message of Confucius to the world, a similar role as John the Baptist had in the history of Christianity. As often happens in life, he was given a nickname, Menci, by his family and friends back in Hainan, but Aisha complicated the situation by calling him Dalai because she thought that he looked like the Dalai Lama. She knew that this was confusing because Menci had never been a Buddhist and was highly unlikely to become one.

Menci was wise, friendly and surprisingly worldly, without in any way detracting from his commitment to Confucius. Importantly to them both, their relationship was not sexual. Not that they weren't physically and emotionally attracted to one another; it just was not on their personal agendas.

Menci helped Aisha along the way to a new religious life that, while not rejecting of Islam, had reached beyond it. She now felt a special calling that would occupy a new compartment in her life, the development of interfaith relationships. This led to them joining and having a role in a local interfaith group, which had as members a wide range of people who were Christian, Jewish, Muslim, Hindu, Sikh, Buddhist, Shinto, Confucian, Bahai, Mormon and Mennonite. Recently, Menci had been elected as the group's leader, a position in which he was thriving.

For Aisha, among her ever-broadening group of medical clients in crises, she was caring for four special people in her professional life, Graeme, Scott, Julia and Jamie. Each lived closer to the edge of eternity than any of her other clients and were in need of her most wise and humane input.

But Aisha faced a series of challenges about how she should handle each one personally and separately. This centred around how she could speak meaningfully to each one of these four human beings, whom were each almost certainly moving into their final days in ways that were far apart. They were starkly unalike, people who were each on different pathways that may never converge. But Aisha wondered how she might best organise a convergence that would have benefit to all concerned. At least she could try to get two of them together, perhaps even three or, if a miracle occurred, all four.

It was worth a try. Indeed, it may yet turn out to be an imperative.

Chapter Three

Graeme Brown left his car where he had parked it, in the backyard of the small building where Aisha's medical practice was located. He would retrieve it sometime. Didn't really matter when. Somehow possessions now seemed inconsequential.

He needed some serious thinking time, and the best way to achieve this would be to walk home, rather slowly and peacefully, eliminating all fear and stress. He chose the longest possible route, which would enable him to enjoy as much fresh air as he could consume as well as feel a sense of freedom in the open spaces of a couple of pleasant parklands. The walk might open up his mind to an extent that he had never before experienced, as he felt a need to spend quality time on acute self-examination and on seriously preparing a plan to die well. He wanted his family to share a genuine experience with him, which would enhance their lives as well as make his departure a special experience for them, not a time of gloom.

Graeme thought of the famous musical Evita and its beautiful theme song 'Don't Cry For Me Argentina'. Maybe he should adapt it to be 'Don't Cry For Me Oh My Family'.

It was vital that, when he spoke to his wife, Penelope, he must have a clear vision of what he should say about his imminent death. What did he feel were the best words to use? He could marry it with what she could determine would be meaningful to her as he walked towards the tolling of the bells. His death would impact her life in ways far more challenging than what would be his experience of it. Maybe it would be more challenging for their twins, Luke and Fiona, who were both just twenty-two years old and in the process of creating great lives via splendid careers.

What was his best starting point in achieving this? What would be most meaningful to all of them? Well, he thought, I will start by not feeling sorry for myself, now or ever. The existence of cancer in his body was in no way unfair. People who suffered from a dreadful ailment called 'poor little me' were an appalling pain in the butt. He had met far too many of them in his experience as a pastor. They yelled abuse at those who would live while they died, claiming that they were lesser beings than them.

He would have to work out how to handle his relationship with friends too, who would not have a clue what to say when he told them that he would be dead in three months. This was mainly due to the fact that they would not have given much thought as to how they would react if they were ever in the same situation that he now faced. Graeme then began to think of how to finally say farewell to as many friends as he could. Their friendship was very important to him, and they would be especially so in the days before he took his final step with voluntary assisted dying, which he wanted to do in the happiest possible way.

His financial affairs would need careful planning too. He had done extraordinarily well from his career as an author, so he had more than a few dollars in the bank plus many sound investments. He would give considerable thought as to how he would distribute his assets wisely before he died. This would require a unanimous family decision as at the time of his death his money would have no value to him whatsoever.

Then there was the crucial issue of what role, if any, the Church would have at his funeral. Would he invite his bishop to conduct the funeral, or would he seek permission for it to be held in a church without the participation of the hierarchy? Would it simply be held at a funeral home or out in a park? At this point, he would prefer the latter. It could involve some delicately tactful planning. So be it.

In his mind, Graeme had never left the Church that Jesus of Nazareth had established. The Church had left him in the same way as it had left Jesus. The crucial thought he had in his ever-active mind at this early stage of his personal crisis was whether he had quite definitely reached the final stage of his theological journey, affirming his extreme doubts about whether or not there was life after death. He had been certain for years that it was a myth. Did he still hold this belief? Did his convictions really matter anyway? And why worry about it right now? But maybe he should at least give the idea the dignity of one last cross-examination.

He was now walking along the bank of the river and was getting home far too quickly. He needed more thinking time. He decided to sit down on the grass under an old tree that had many branches and much foliage. It would be a pleasant spot for reflection, and he rested his back against the tree trunk, quietly analysing and reviewing his life. Hopefully, the gentle breeze drifting in from the peacefully flowing water would clear his mind and grant him some much-needed clarity of thought, as well as a sense of peace and some assurance that his life had in some small way benefited the needs of humanity.

It quietly occurred to him that, as he came closer to death, he was finally beginning to understand what life actually means.

The scene was now set for Graeme to ask himself a tough question. Had he ever really achieved anything of significance in his life, something that would have a lasting meaning for those with whom he would soon be separated, let alone the world itself?

Perhaps he should pause now to reflect on and review the highlights and dark spaces of his life. Yes, this would be a good starting point. His parents, Angus and Margaret, who had long since passed away, had been fine people with a strong Christian commitment. They gave him every opportunity to make something significant of his life. They were hardworking Anglo-Saxon protestants, staunch Presbyterians in fact, who had lived at the lower level of the middle class and had led a simple, wholesome, peaceful life, which enabled him to grow up without facing any significant crises.

His parents saved mightily to ensure that he got a good-quality education at a prestigious Church School that charged solid fees. This was followed by an arts degree at the local university named after St. Andrew. The next step was to gain admission to an ecumenical Theological College that focused on progressive Christian values. All the way, his parents supported him financially, an act of love and commitment for which he was enormously grateful and which he was now repaying by giving the same loving commitment to his own children.

Graeme's sole regret throughout his stable family life was that he was an only child. Margaret had had considerable difficulty with his birth, and this put an end to any future childbearing. This meant that he did not have the experience of sharing things with brothers and sisters, but his parents made up for this by teaching him to be a generous giver and a committed voluntary worker who always, by instinct, involved himself in great human causes.

A huge moment in his time at Theological College was his decision to change from being Presbyterian and to join the Anglicans. It had been a tough call but an essential one for him. In his formative years, he gradually became disenchanted with fundamentalist Christianity. It just did not ring true. He felt that it was the realm of insecure people who wanted certainty in their lives, but there was no such thing in life as certainty—except for the certainty that there was God and that a man called Jesus of Nazareth was worth following.

Even though there was a liberal wing of the Presbyterian Church, Graeme found its commitment to change too slow and tentative, always trying to not upset people by only making slight changes to the status quo.

He sought a radical faith that was much stronger than this. The Anglo-Catholic wing of the Anglican Church seemed to provide this opening. There were theologians in it who were constantly searching for meaning and purpose.

So after many long talks with Angus and Margaret, he made the change from Presbyterian to Anglican. They were perplexed, but they trusted his integrity as well as his sincerity and his ever-searching mind, so they went along with it. Steadily, they warmed to it, but remained staunchly Presbyterian themselves.

When Graeme achieved his Bachelor of Theology, in addition to a Bachelor of Arts, he was fortunate to be called directly from college to become rector of an Anglican parish in an affluent community, without being required to serve time somewhere as an assistant priest while he learned the basic skills of ministry. This appointment enabled him to walk in influential circles that had access to powerful people with connections to the corridors of power. It often led to him having meetings with the great and the mighty.

He had natural gifts that helped him make a good impression as he scaled the ladder of life. He was tall and slim with a magnificent head of red hair that made him stand out at all gatherings. Added to this was a natural ability to get on with people, be articulate, and achieve success as a humble motivator. He looked and acted like a fellow who was going places.

Unfortunately, he gained little fulfilment from his work, and had a feeling of being constantly under pressure to observe dogma and tradition, which meant that he was constantly required to advocate elements of the faith about which he held no genuine conviction. His own views on the inadequacy of dogmas and creeds had been clearly expressed during his years at Theological College. But he had found that no matter whether they were professors or students, few were interested in getting actively involved in such a debate, as they worried that any controversy would impede their careers in the Church.

Graeme held huge doubts about what were regarded as the cornerstones of the faith, such as included the existence of Heaven and Hell, a Creator God, the Virgin Birth, the Resurrection, the Ascension, Eternal Life, the Second Coming of Christ and the Forgiveness of Sins. Even more radically, he could not accept that Jesus died for our sins. He believed that Jesus died to give us life. He was also disillusioned by the Church itself and its selfish tradition of ensuring its own survival at all costs while not putting resources into the advancement of Christianity in the community.

Nevertheless, Graeme did achieve a number of positive things during his parish ministry, and he felt a justifiable degree of pride in them. He founded a community service organisation called ACTS, which he legally registered as a national charity. He raised the majority of its funds from the congregation over and above their Sunday offerings, and those funds were distributed as grants directly to people beyond his parish who were going through tough times. Most of them weren't churchgoers, and many were refugees or migrants or victims of domestic violence and elder abuse. At the time that he left the parish, it was giving away at least $100,000 each year and growing in size and scope annually. His successors as parish priest kept it going and were doing their best to expand it.

Then he had started a personal movement called Pilgrims. It involved people who undertook to, at least once a month, find someone who had real personal problems, either financial or otherwise, and quietly help them, not necessarily financially but certainly in opening doors to influential people who could help them find a better pathway in life. You became a Pilgrim only by personal invitation from Graeme. You were usually a casual Christian who turned up only at Christmas and Easter or at funerals. In other words, the non-biblebashers. There were now one hundred Pilgrims. The gender of Pilgrims was roughly fifty-fifty, and he ensured that some were gay and lesbian. All came from a variety of races and cultures and religions. He especially invited some atheists.

Greame kept in touch with them all and invited them to have breakfast with him at the Church Hall several times a year, with all Pilgrims tossing a banknote in a bowl to cover breakfast costs. The breakfasts were forums that discussed the needs of society at large and provided ideas for Pilgrims to find new people in need. When he left the parish, the Pilgrims unanimously invited him to remain in their ranks, and he did, carefully doing at least one good deed a month.

He was especially proud of a group of a dozen lawyers whom he invited to work with him on matters of social justice. He enlisted them mainly from out of the community, not from his own Church, but two of them were members of his Church who would keep the congregation informed of what was being achieved without breaching confidentiality. He gave the lawyers the title of Crusaders.

They did not take part in any public marches or unlawful assemblies. They found people who were unjustly treated by their employers, whether from the underpayment of wages or wrongful dismissal. Women who were denied equality or suffered sexual harassment. Minorities who were denied basic human rights. All work was done pro bono. If those whom they helped wanted to pay for the services they had received, they were invited to make a gift to ACTS.

All of the above gave Graeme powerful reasons to get out of bed every morning, but there were still gaps in his life.

——————

These activities were regarded by some Church leaders as not traditional Church activities that resembled those of the political left. Add to this Graeme's radical theology and it led to regular rifts between him and the deans, archdeacons, bishops and archbishops to whom he was finally responsible and was expected to show unquestioning support and respect.

It led also to regularly recurring tensions with the fundamentalists and traditionalists who formed a significant part of his own congregation, most of whom were following the faith they had learned in Sunday school and from which they never grew. The simplicity of it made their lives so happily peaceful, and any changes that would disturb that peace should wait until after their funerals.

Matters came to a head when Graeme preached a controversial sermon in the cathedral, which he gave the long title of 'God does not forgive sins that we don't make amends for'. It was the occasion of the annual Synod of the Diocese attended by delegates from all the parishes, and Graeme had been invited to give what they called the occasional address.

He had for many years stopped using in public worship the words 'Your sins are forgiven'. He believed that it was cowardly for any Christian to hurt another person and then seek God's forgiveness without apologising to that person and making recompense for that sin.

In the cathedral that day, he went further and called on the Church to stop forgiving paedophiles and rapists who kept on sinning because they knew that, on the next Sunday, they could be certain they would be forgiven, and every Sunday thereafter as well. He said that the entire matter represented gross hypocrisy by the Church. He named no individuals as guilty, and spoke quietly, sincerely and persuasively. Many in the congregation were warmly supportive, but the bishop had been aghast. One of the lynchpins of his reign was his power to forgive, or not forgive, on God's behalf. This was treason.

His Grace confronted Graeme that very day and informed him that he was terminating Graeme's ministry in his parish and would arrange for him to serve elsewhere. This happened on the tenth anniversary of his arrival in the parish. It was all done relatively pleasantly, but he was given no option in the matter. He decided not to contest it as it would divide the congregation of his parish unnecessarily.

On his final Sunday, it took five separate services, rather than the normal three, to handle the crowds of well-wishers. Most were there to applaud his outstanding ministry, but some turned up to rejoice his departure.

With the clear intention of keeping him out of the public eye, the bishop offered him a five-year appointment as a hospital chaplain.

Graeme and Penelope thought about it deeply and decided it would give him a peaceful base within the Church from where he could launch a new career, which he was already planning as an author. He found that the role of chaplain genuinely created a real niche in his spiritual life from which he could meet the personal needs of people, rather than entertain them with trendy sermons. In particular, it enabled him to help people live and die well. It would grow to become the core of his spiritual life and a base from which he could provide real leadership in spreading the faith.

Now, he felt with certainty that his experience as a chaplain would give him the spiritual power to handle his own death well.

In terms of daily activity, his work as a chaplain gave Graeme extra time to expand his skills for his new vocation as an author. He had already made a name for himself as a controversial opinion writer for religious newspapers and magazines, so he expanded his thinking and took the next logical step. He wrote his first novel and named it the intriguing title *Leo's Light*.

The book was based on the life of an extremely radical Roman Catholic priest who had been named Leo, as this had been a popular title for several popes who had taken up the name of Leo down the centuries. History has subsequently proved that being called Leo was not really an honour, as most of those famous Leos had been quite decadent. One was charged by King Charlemagne with adultery and perjury and other sins too plentiful to mention.

In Graeme's novel, the modern Leo has the fortunate fate of being defrocked by a highly conservative cardinal. This event gives him the opportunity to live as a high-profile and public communicator, and he becomes a huge critic of the Church and its inflexible dogmas. Leo is finally murdered by a brutal conservative fanatic acting on clear instructions from the Lord. This makes him and his controversial writing even more popular.

Graeme's clear purpose in writing the book was to create debate about whether you ever needed to be involved in a Church if you wanted to be a Christian. He went overboard in declaring that Churches were a hindrance along your pathway to the faith. This added huge fuel to the fires of his life.

So it was that Graeme's first venture as an author created a book that sold like hotcakes, well over 250,000 copies, and set him on a path to literary fame. Years later, it still sold steadily. Half a dozen more popular books followed. His second was about a highly respected conservative cardinal who is elected pope on the basis of the immense respect with which he is held by the Church worldwide. After settling quietly into his new role, he announces that he will remove the requirement that priests and nuns must be celibate. He will also allow women to become priests and will have no restrictions placed on their eligibility to fulfil any role in the Church. This meant that one day there could be a female pope. Predictably, he is forced to resign as the result of a hugely political coup within the Vatican, which creates a worldwide rift in the Church. He is demoted to the role of parish priest and sent to a remote part of the world where he begins to perform astonishing miracles of healing, the story of which hits the media. The ramifications are so enormous that after his death he is nominated to be canonised as a saint, thereby creating more turmoil.

This book sold even better than the first. It hit a real nerve among nominal Christians everywhere. More books followed, and each had an interesting background of religion, ethics and morals. Graeme achieved a stature as the conscience of the community worldwide.

Recently, his latest book outsold the rest. It featured a devoted nun who gave up her vows and left the Church saying she had lost her faith. In reality, she was the victim of a bishop who was a sexual predator and who constantly violated her against her will after causing severe physical and mental injuries. The Vatican, as usual, covers up for the bishop, decreeing that she be banished from attending any church anywhere and denied the eucharist permanently. Eventually, she marries a powerful Jewish member of parliament who decides to organise revenge on her behalf by getting the huge injustice reversed.

He does so in a high-profile speech to a crowded parliament and a packed press gallery and shakes the Church all the way to the pope, who tries to run for cover and fails, swamped by a universally hostile social media.

As would be expected, these huge successes led Graeme further and further away from his chosen vocation as an Anglican priest. He did not renounce his ordination vows, as he wanted to retain the right to return one day—even though his bishop at that time seemed to be overjoyed that Graeme's fame was, for the foreseeable future, keeping him out of the Church's leadership circles. The bishop prayed that this would remain so until he could retire.

Graeme's fame also led his life in another direction, this time to a well-paid contract out in the secular world. A large regional bank retained his services as their ethics adviser. He was surprised when they approached him, as working for a bank was something far from his mind. They wanted a person of independence and integrity to lead them in enhancing their market share in areas of life far from the conventional territory of the big banks. The regional bank not only sought to achieve a permanent image as good guys, they genuinely wanted to be good guys and invest heavily to enhance society.

So Graeme set out to create a closely bonded family of shareholders, directors, managers, staff, contractors and customers who previously had no contact with one another and who would work happily together to pioneer positive changes in community values, as well as to ensure that the bank was personally and permanently involved as a legitimate partner in society.

He enjoyed this work and the many challenges associated with it. It also brought him into a world in which Churches had no tangible prior involvement. It proved to him that Churches that remained locked in religious buildings far removed from the needs of humanity, and that always endeavoured to save itself as an institution, had no future. He aimed to change this.

Graeme pondered how he would convey to the chief executive of the bank that he would not be able to complete his assignment now, due to circumstances beyond his control, but how he could ensure that his work continued and expanded. The thought filled his soul with both sadness and gladness.

Well, the sun was setting rapidly in more ways than one. He was aware that he needed to turn it into a beautiful sunset.

———•———

Graeme broke from his meditations and rose from under the tree at the riverbank, walking steadily homewards so as to be with Penelope as soon as possible. He was ready to tell her his news. If there's any virtue in impending death, it's that it focused your mind, so you find yourself thinking and speaking in the present tense.

Penelope had been in the crowd on the very first Sunday of his ministry in his first and only parish. In the middle of his inaugural sermon, he had seen her sitting in one of the back rows of the church. He stopped momentarily in his tracks and took a second look. The congregation thought he was just pausing before making a dramatic punchline.

'That's her,' he said to himself.

He almost forgot where he was in the sermon, but quickly regained his composure and went on as planned. At the church door, when he was steadily shaking hands with his new flock for the first time, she eventually reached the top of the line. He held her hand for a wee bit longer than the rest of them.

'I am Penelope,' she said.

'Good morning, Penelope, it's a pleasure to meet you.'

She gave him a nice smile and moved on as there was still a long queue behind her. It was the start of a wonderful relationship, one for the ages. And it had led to this moment, when he would tell her that it was coming to an end.

He opened the front door of their lovely home and was, as always, greeted warmly by Penelope.

'What good news did Aisha give you today? Are you still making steady progress?'

'She told me I will be dead in three months.'

She knew him so well that she immediately knew he was not joking.

For a moment, her heart stopped beating.

Chapter Four

Scott had totally forgotten about his urgent second Covid-19 test, as the very thought of it was utter nonsense. It was a trivial nuisance that had no right whatsoever to hold up God's unmistakeable destiny for him. It was the equivalent of blasphemy, and so he had excluded it from his mind and was instead concentrating on important issues that were clearly God's will.

His phone rang, emitting its carefully selected holy sound. All calls were heralded by the first line of his favourite hymn, 'Onward, Christian Soldiers'. He was on the frontline with those soldiers and would be there forever. He would lead every charge in the defence of righteousness. It had nothing to do with ego, it was simply a fact.

Aisha's name was showing on the screen.

'More nonsense,' he whispered to himself. Then without a greeting, he said in a relatively friendly tone, slightly above the level of the cold conservations he normally had with people whom, with huge paternalism, he regarded as servants, 'You are about to confirm what I already know deep in my soul. I am negative for Covid-19, always have been and always will be.'

'To the contrary, Mr Palmer, I am confirming what I told you just a few hours ago. You are Covid-19 positive, and, unfortunately, the initial evidence is that you have a highly contagious variant of the virus that could be a clear threat to your life if we do not respond to it quickly. My firm recommendation is that you must go into immediate isolation in hospital and receive the best possible treatment before it is too late.'

'I will not go to any hospital anywhere. God protects me. However, I agree that I should remain here in isolation in my own home until this bad case of the flu can be cleared up.'

'This is a very unfortunate decision on your part, Mr Palmer. I now have no option under the health laws of our nation but to report your case immediately to the Centre for Infectious Diseases as an infection that not only puts your own life in danger, but also means that you are a considerable threat to your own family, as well as a danger to your friends and neighbours. I will ask them to send an ambulance within the hour to bring you to hospital.'

'I will not get into any ambulance.'

'I will advise them of your attitude and strongly recommend to them that it will be necessary to arrange for a police officer to come to your home with the ambulance to ensure that you go to hospital.'

He was now angry. Close to being out of control. 'Don't stand over me with wild threats,' he said. 'You are a typical panicking female as well as a non-believer in the Lord. I know that I do not have coronavirus. God would have revealed it to me if I did. He will not allow anything to impede my calling to achieve the incredible visions He has set for me. He simply will not.'

'Can we talk with God later? Right now, I have a civic responsibility to ensure that you get to hospital as a matter of urgency, and I have no doubt that your God will back my decision.'

'My front door is locked and I will not open it to anyone.'

'I will advise the police of your attitude and inform them that they may need to force their way in. I will recommend that they should bring with them a warrant for your arrest and confinement for breaking health laws and being a danger to the health of society.'

'This is an outrage. I find it unbelievably difficult to comprehend why you are doing this to me.'

'It is nothing of the sort. It is a battle with death. Your life and the lives of others near you. You are irresponsibly putting their lives in danger.'

'You are from this moment not my doctor. Please remove yourself from all actions you are implementing on my behalf, as you have no authority to carry them out.'

'You have my resignation as of this moment. This clears the decks for me to now ask the state government to appoint a police doctor in my place. You will have no say in who it is.'

'May God have mercy on your soul.'

'He will. I can feel his presence in my soul right now.'

Aisha was the one who disconnected the call. She sat back in her chair in disbelief and disappointment. Did the God whom Christians worship actually require them to be selfish and irresponsible and quite stupid? Strange God.

She reached out to pick up her phone so that she could pass Scott Palmer over to the long arm of the law.

<hr>

Scott's anger grew to an even greater intensity, which simply aggravated his constant coughing. He was experiencing increasing trouble in breathing, and his behaviour was spiralling out of control with each passing second. Suddenly, his distress turned to panic. He whispered the words of Jesus on the Cross.

'My God, why have you forsaken me?'

God did not reply. So Scott called Pauline, and she did. He told her the unpleasant news and waited for her reaction. Pauline had been part of his life for just ten years, and they had no family. One of them had problems with their ability to produce an heir, but they had not yet taken time to find out who it was. However, they were discussing seriously when and how they could adopt a refugee orphan.

Pauline had private wealth and was aware of her need to conserve and grow it responsibly. She was also conscious of the role of money in her Christian life and used it carefully and sparingly as a good Christian is supposed to do.

It was at a church dance that Scott had met her. He was immediately attracted, and the feeling was mutual. This attraction was enhanced when he subsequently found that she had money, much more than him at that stage. Their wedding was quite an event, as her generous parents spared no expense. It had everything you could expect at a grand wedding, except alcohol. The religious beliefs of all four of them banned it. You got high on the Holy Spirit, not inferior spirits like whisky. Nor even wine, despite Jesus having partaken of it at the marriage feast at Cana.

Pauline invested, conservatively, in most of Scott's business ventures and was serving on the boards of directors of some of them, the ones whose goals interested her. A few of them did not. She was not as passionate about the Prosperity Gospel as he was because she held the view that, while it was acceptable in God's sight for a Christian to be wealthy, it should not be flaunted, as it was a private financial arrangement with God. Friends often wondered if it was actually possible to be more publicly enthusiastic about being financially successful in business than Scott was.

As was to be expected, her private investments were always made without risk as she did her homework very carefully. She loved the Lord but did not totally trust his business acumen. She did believe, however, that it was more likely you would earn more money by working with Him, rather than by ignoring him. However, for her it was never the obsession that it was for her husband.

Now she and Scott faced a personal crisis. Covid-19 had invaded their lives when, by the will of God, it had no place there. Pauline's first reaction was to be more belligerent than he was, assuring him that she was prepared to guard the front door with a steak knife in hand to let intruders know that God was in charge, and that she was His powerful and determined representative who would carry out His will without hesitation.

Yet she began to discover that a few frightening realities were creeping into her conservative mind, calling for decisive action on her part. If Scott did have Covid-19, and if it was the variant that Aisha had outlined, then she too was in trouble. Scott had been coughing in her presence for a couple of days, and she shared a bed with him. Neither of them had thought about wearing a mask or observing physical distancing.

She decided that it would be wise if she took some decisive steps to protect herself. In reality, she wanted to take control of the situation just to show Scott that he was not always entitled to call all the shots. She was of a mind that the time had come for her to break out of the faithful wife image.

'Scott,' she said, 'if you have a virulent case of the virus, then I am almost certain to get it also. I think that you had better go to hospital as a sensible precaution for us both. There is nothing to be gained by taking unnecessary risks. As soon as you are on the way there, I will make an urgent call to Aisha and arrange for me to be quickly tested here at home today. At the very least, this means I will have to self-isolate until I get the results. It may mean that I will have to go to hospital too. In the meantime, we will keep in touch by phone. This is just a hurdle that has unexpectedly appeared along the way in our journey with Jesus to enhance his kingdom.'

'I have just fired Aisha for incompetence and creating unnecessary panic, so you had better make other arrangements.'

'This is unfortunate. You have given me no option but to apologise and reinstate her. This is no time for us to be changing doctors. Besides which, you and I like her. So I had better pack your bag for you to take for your stay in hospital. You will only be there for a few days at the most. You should put your computer and phone and papers and anything else you may need into your briefcase so you can keep working for the Lord.'

Scott was feeling so poorly that he decided it would be wisest if he followed her advice, much as he disagreed with it.

'I know that our Lord will be leading you in your thinking, Pauline, so I will follow His guidance. Although I am unsure of where He is leading us at this important moment in our lives. This obstacle has come out of nowhere and has shaken me to the depths of my soul. I am lost in the wilderness.'

'Me too. But we both know that we can't argue with God.'

Nevertheless, Scott's mind was in turmoil, and his jumbled thoughts led him to reflect on his journey through his life to reach this point.

———

Scott had come from a broken home. His parents despised one another and involved themselves in regular acts of domestic violence, alternatively originating from both sides. They stuck together supposedly because of him. He really had no alternative but to flee from this appalling environment when he was in his early teens.

He had self-educated and dragged himself up the ladder of life by taking one tough step after the other, often hanging on by his teeth and his bootlaces. Then a friend took him to a meeting of the Presbyterian Young People's Fellowship. He liked the people he met there. They accepted him without any questions about his past. He felt he belonged, so he stayed on with growing enthusiasm.

Scott followed his passion for self-education by reading many religious books, particularly religious novels as they focussed on the reality of life, not difficult theology. One that really impressed him was a century-old novel called *The Robe*, written by the legendary American Lutheran minister Lloyd Douglas, who had millions of readers back in the days before World War II.

The Robe is the wonderful tale of Marcellus, a Roman soldier who was ordered by Pontius Pilate to carry out the crucifixion of Jesus. Marcellus took back to his room the robe that Jesus wore that day. Its close presence changed his life. He went out to find and meet with followers of Jesus to discover what fired them up so passionately. Everyone of them told him that, as the result of their life with Jesus, they had given up all their old habits and had found a wonderful new life that was worth living. They were profoundly happy and fearless.

Scott's fascination with this book led him to a great moment when he, for the first time, seriously encountered Jesus of Nazareth in a real and meaningful way. It happened at a church camp that he attended. A fellow from the farmlands, whose experience of life was similar to his, led a discussion on how to be a genuine Christian by making Jesus your role model. Scott bought that real big. The old chains fell off. His life was transformed. He had the new life that Marcellus had discovered two thousand years previously.

Not long afterwards, one of the more confident members of the PFA introduced him to the theology of the Prosperity Gospel. It gripped him. God meant for him to be rich. This fact mesmerised him. God looked after those who followed him without question. Scott read all that he could about the idea and put it into practice. It worked, for him anyway. It never occurred to him to check on how many people had tried to practice it but had failed and were too afraid to admit it. Nor did he ever think about or debate whether it was true or false that God had a grand design for the whole world. More rational people would have felt that if He did have a plan, He was taking a long time to bring it to reality.

Even so, Scott did discover that it was the Pentecostal Church that was the powerhouse of the Prosperity Gospel, so he left the Presbyterians and joined them as he knew that he must work closely with the true believers if he was to achieve the maximum success that God intended for him.

One of his newfound Pentecostal friends introduced him to an eminent sharebroker who attended the same church. Soon this led to a job offer, and his career as a share trader blossomed through a combination of hard work and an unshakeable belief in his prosperous destiny. After staying with the stockbroking firm for a respectable number of years, he decided to launch out on his own.

His decision to do his own thing was largely driven by his over-awareness that he was short in stature and not at all stocky. This meant that he suffered from small-man syndrome, i.e., he had a constant need to prove to himself and the world that he was just as good, even better, than the big guys.

In addition, he was confident that God was with him every inch of the way. He had prospered well, and he started establishing private equity companies with striking success in several areas of commerce and industry. He became a person of genuine note in the world of finance and a role model for aspiring young guys.

A huge element of his success was that he always employed young Christians whom he had introduced to the Prosperity Gospel. Most of them bought the philosophy big time. His company became a spiritual powerhouse. No goal was too awesome. God was always there as the cornerstone of it all. There was never any fear.

He was on the brink of greatness. It was so close. There was no way that it could fail now. Covid-19 was a minor diversion.

Then this very year, God had led Scott to undertake an important and visionary goal. The Lord led him well into the planning phase of establishing a boutique university, which would be privately owned and have just one faculty based solely on teaching the Prosperity Gospel.

One of its ground-breaking ventures would be to foster the neglected concept of not-for-profit companies, which had always been around but not pushed by anyone with any intent to take them into the mainstream. Scott's plan was to use them to create innovative industries by combining graduate studies with in-depth research into the widest range of possibilities.

These innovative companies would have no shareholders, only subscribers who had a small fixed liability for debts. In Scott's vision, all employees would be practising Christians and would be paid significant salaries that gave them a regular stream of private wealth that they could invest privately and wisely. No bonuses or dividends would be paid to anyone. Profits would be used in two ways. Half would be ploughed back into the development of the company so it would become even more profitable and pay even better salaries. The other half would go into a foundation associated solely with the company and which funded Christian causes.

In Scott's call to the faith, he would serve his God in spectacular fashion, using his business skills to foster these companies so they would become powerhouses to finance the growth of Christianity, and he would set moral and ethical standards for the honest operation of the companies. In addition, he would destroy socialism as a core practice of economics by creating this new sharing version of modern capitalism, which would spread wealth among many as an alternative to raising living standards by government handouts.

He knew that his God hated socialists and did not want any of them in his flock. They were fundamentally lazy people who did not use their God-given talents. They loafed on the goodwill of Christians. He would make a huge effort to destroy them.

The first of these new companies was about to be launched using the new university as its base. It would concentrate on new ways of using the waste created by humanity to create energy in the cheapest-possible form for consumers.

Right now, Scott was needed on the frontline of the promotional strategy to get it off the ground safely and well. But Covid-19 had now denied his leadership that these ventures needed. He was at a total loss as to why God had allowed this to happen. During his devout and constant prayers, God had assured him that He wanted it all to happen right now. The current situation was devastating. What had he done to let God down and displease Him?

Was it due to the deadly virus outbreak at his church? He and Pauline had been away on holidays when it happened and had not participated in the decision, but they agreed with it as they too believed that God cared for His own and therefore there was no need for the Church to obey the virus restrictions. The consequences were dreadful, even though it had been done as an act of sincere faith.

There was a knock at the door. Pauline answered the summons and invited the paramedics and police to come in. They were covered in protective gear but declined to enter, saying that the house was now infected. They asked Scott to come to the door where they gave him a mask to wear and invited him to get into a wheelchair they had brought, so that he could sit comfortably isolated in the rear of the ambulance separated from them by a wall.

Scott waved goodbye to Pauline, as he was asked not to embrace her, and then did as he was told to expedite his journey to hospital. The police clearly and firmly instructed Pauline not to leave the house under any circumstances for fourteen days, unless it was for the sole purpose of being admitted to hospital. All food and other items must be delivered and left outside her door. The police said that they would arrange with Dr Jinnah for a government pathologist to visit her within the hour to take a Covid-19 test. They would also arrange for the house, yard and vehicles to be deep-cleaned that very day. All of this left Pauline in a growing state of unease, but she nodded assent.

Scott looked back at Pauline and his home as the ambulance drove him away. For the first time, it dawned on him that it was possible he may never see either of them again. His total confidence, that had always affirmed him as someone special, was beginning to shatter. It was utterly unbelievable that neither he nor God were in charge of this ridiculous situation. It was imperative that he, and God, regained control of his life immediately.

Chapter Five

Jessie Windsor walked purposefully through the park. She knew that she should not be doing this, as the darkness of night had settled in and the streetlights were remote. But she was running late for a meeting with a friend at her nearby home, so she took the risk.

Jessie had been taking risks for all her eighty-nine years, and had gone through many tough experiences with lots of odd and difficult people, surviving every one of them. She could cope with another one if it occurred. So why worry? Armed as usual with a torch and a mace spray, she felt secure, so she had no real qualms about giving it a go. Life always provided challenges that bring out a few feelings of inadequacy, so that actually created an exciting world. Most people tried to be nice to little old ladies anyway.

As a precaution, she swept the glow of her torch around the trees and bushes as she walked steadily onwards along the broad pathway. She did not want any molesters to think that she was unaware of her circumstances or that she was in any way unprepared for them.

Suddenly, she heard a sharp, loud cry. It didn't sound like a bird or animal. Must be human, she thought. She stopped and flashed her torch in the direction of the sound. Transfixed, she was aghast at the sight she beheld a few metres beside the track.

A person was lying on the grass beside one of the park benches. It was a woman. What a dangerously exposed place to sleep, Jessie thought. She looked closer. My God, a knife lay on the grass beside her. Cautiously, she went closer still. There was a substance on the grass. It looked like blood. Shocked, Jessie studied the immediate surroundings to make sure a killer wasn't lurking before moving quickly towards the woman. She was very still, except Jessie saw that the woman was sobbing, and that her distress was such that she appeared to be in a state of panic.

Both the woman's wrists were slashed, but, seemingly, not all that badly. Jessie reached out to feel the pulse on the arm closest to where the knife lay. It was not strong, but it gave an indication of hope that not too much blood had yet flowed.

Regaining her composure, Jessie took her phone from her handbag and dialled the emergency number. Using the minimum number of words possible, she gave her location and described the scene, expressing her opinion as an old grandma, who had reared six children and helped bring up fifteen grandchildren, that she felt that the life before her would more likely end in minutes not hours if help did not arrive. She firmly asserted that they should act with urgent speed.

Jessie then did her best to staunch the flow of blood and decided that she must continue to do all she can while she waited, but the contents of her handbag did not contain anything of real use. She deliberately left the knife where it was and carefully kept away from the park bench, as both may be crucial sources of evidence of whatever had happened here.

Her 'patient' appeared to have no sign of other injuries. Nor was there any evidence of a struggle. In Jessie's amateur view as the local Miss Marple, it looked as though this may be an attempted suicide. Perplexed, the woman made no attempt whatsoever to speak to Jessie and was not trying to get up or help herself in any way.

After asking what had happened and getting no response, Jessie decided that it was pointless to try to start a conversation. This person seemed to be in a state of confusion and disorientation. A couple of times the woman mumbled,

'I am sorry.' But Jessie could not work out whom she was apologising to. The woman had enough strength to keep trying to reach for the knife, as if she was making an effort to use it again. Jessie restrained her, as the victim had no more business with that knife, and, in her view, it was not wise to disturb whatever evidence that knife held. Maybe the woman was trying to hide it.

Jessie regretted that she did not have a bottle of water in her bag, and she could not see a tap nearby. She had no doubt that this woman needed to drink lots of it.

After what seemed an interminable length of time, the paramedics arrived on the scene, hotly followed by the police. After a swift examination and staunching of the blood flow, as well as questions of Jessie as to what had happened, the paramedics took the stricken woman away at high speed. The police stayed behind to speak further with Jessie, who in reality could tell them little. She did not even know the victim's name, and the police had not had the opportunity to find any identification details on her person, so it was all a bit pointless.

One police officer offered to drive Jessie home, while the other called for help in establishing a crime scene. But Jessie declined, explaining that she lived not far away. She identified herself as an old pensioner who was happily living out her final days alone in her little cottage. She asked if she could phone the police officer in the morning to find out what finally happened to this sad person. He readily agreed and they exchanged contact details.

Something told her that she should not lose contact with this woman who seemed to be in a lonely and confused wilderness at a critical moment in her life. In addition, the panicked look on the woman's face had given Jessie the feeling that she did not really want to die.

If no one had tried to kill her, why then did she try to do it herself? Something was strange about the entire event. Maybe she could help this sad soul somehow. She had been doing it for years with lots of people she did not really know all that well.

The call from the police just a few moments ago added yet another crisis to Aisha's life. However, this was the vocation she had chosen, and she accepted it without complaint or regret.

She drove quickly to the hospital and headed directly to the emergency department, where she knew a medical team were in the process of saving the life of Julia Hawke, who had only recently become one of Aisha's many patients.

It would have been an understatement for Aisha to have described Julia as a difficult person to deal with, either medically or socially. From the start of their first consultation, it was clear that Julia's life was a highly emotional exercise founded on a lot of negativity and stress, mostly self-inflicted. Clearly she suffered from fractured relationships with many people, which led to prolonged depression, eating disorders, insecure employment and insufficient money to pay basic debts. These dominating features of her life combined to make her a very unstable person, even on the best days.

But Aisha had not considered her to be suicidal. She thought of Julia as someone who often thrived on her own suffering. This generated a severe attack of that appalling disease called 'poor little me', as well as a huge lump of ridiculous negativity. And she was an atheist—at least, she said she was, but Aisha held the view that Julia had just added God to her long list of enemies.

This did not cause a problem for Aisha, but this likely meant that Julia had no basic belief system that would lay a foundation for the restoration of her life to some basic level of normality. But then Aisha had never studied atheism. She had met atheists, and some appeared to have a confident and self-assured attitude. But she was not yet sure as to whether that had penetrated to any real depth below the surface of their public persona.

An intensive care nurse on duty gave her Julia's file. It was clear that when the ambulance had brought in Julia, the doctors working that night had saved her life. They had begun by restoring her blood level and repairing her wounds, but as she was in a state of almost total confusion, she was put under sedation. Strangely, the photographs of Julia's wounds clearly showed that she had not damaged crucial arteries in her wrists. She had made lots of cuts everywhere except the places that might have killed her.

Aisha went to the cubicle where Julia lay and quietly assessed her situation. Though she was sleeping, she still retained a look of agitation. It was deeply ingrained within her.

The surgeon's written report clearly supported Aisha's view that Julia was alive because she had botched slashing her wrists. Aisha wondered if Julia had deliberately missed her prime arteries. It would not surprise her, as there was usually nothing rational nor predictable about Julia's thought processes.

There was nothing more that Aisha could do. Julia was in competent hands. She would survive, and Aisha could go about her work without any further concern until the hospital advised that Julia was going home. Then she could take over and set about supervising the recovery process. It would be far more mental than physical in its challenge.

Aisha took a look at the paramedic's report regarding what had happened in the park, and this posed more questions. These comments were supported by a report the police had emailed to the hospital. Why had Julia chosen that public park when there was a far more secluded one near her home, which would have allowed her to kill herself without much possibility of being interrupted? There was also the question of why she had cried out, but then did not respond to questions raised by the woman who came to help her. Well, this was the normal Julia.

As Aisha handed the file back to the nurse after recording details of her visit, she asked, 'Who called emergency to report that Julia had tried to take her own life?'

'A nice old lady,' the nurse said. 'I have the details in our police file. They also sent me a copy of their report. I will take a look.'

'Thank you.'

'Her name is Jessie Windsor.'

'Can you give me her contact details?'

'Certainly. I have them right here. May I suggest that at the very least someone should thank her? There cannot be the slightest doubt that she did her best to ensure that Julia got help.'

'I will make sure that happens.'

Aisha drove home with a troubled mind about a vital question. Had Julia really wanted to be saved?

The following day when her work was complete, Aisha called Jessie's number. There was a prompt and friendly answer. After introductions and explanations, Aisha thanked Jessie for her impressive response to her shocking discovery of an unknown woman trying to kill herself in a park. She asked Jessie to give her opinion of Julia's mental state, if any, when Jessie discovered her.

'It was a difficult scene to accurately get a handle on what was happening, Dr Jinnah. I had the feeling that she did not want to die, and that the whole event was a cry for help. But it was a very irresponsible and reckless way to stage a cry for help. Quite crazy actually.'

'I think that your observations are close to the truth. She has always had great difficulty in discovering that there is any real reason to live, but she most probably cannot bring herself to accept that death will be any better.'

'What was her mental state when you last saw her as a patient?'

'Without giving away any confidential medical information, I can say that she was her usual self, very negative about herself and vindictive about those whom she considered responsible for the state of her life. For a long time, she has believed that life is pointless, but I did not get the impression that she was suicidal.'

Jessie had a theory on the matter. 'I had difficulty in communicating with her in any way, as she was sobbing most of the time. But I got the impression that she had deliberately sought my attention. Maybe if she wanted to die, she also did not want to die alone. Her words throughout my short stay with her were hard to work out, except that she kept repeating that she was sorry. But I could not work out why she should be apologising to me when she had done nothing to hurt or threaten me, except to stop me from getting home on time. If she wanted to die, why didn't she ask me to leave her alone and insist that I should get out of the park? I am wondering if she deliberately waited for someone like me to come along the pathway before cutting her wrists.'

'When she recovers, would you be willing to take the time to meet with her?'

'Only if she invites me, and is not doing so because she feels compelled to say something to thank me.'

'I will casually drop it into my next conversation with her. We shall see if she shows any willingness to take it up. But, for the moment, may I ask what your occupation has been in your earlier life?'

'I was a cleaner in a bank, and I was a good cleaner. When I got married, they told me the bank did not employ married women. They were primitive days back then. So I became a full-time mum, and I very much enjoyed it even though I did not have much money to do the job properly.'

'My first thoughts are that Julia could decide that you are just the sort of person who might understand her.'

'Well, occasionally I do prove able to add a little value to some strange situations, so I might as well give this one a go.'

Chapter Six

Jamie had overcome many highs and lows in his memorable life. Born in the Highlands of Scotland, where his family owned a small farm, he received only a basic education, as that was all a person destined to be a farmer was supposed to need.

So it was that when his eldest brother inherited the farm after their father died, a fact of inheritance written into Scottish law, he decided to leave the land of his birth and seek his fortune in another nation. He settled in quickly to his new life and became an apprentice plumber, and eventually started his own plumbing business. He kept it small and did well, because he looked after his customers as if they were family. Along the way, he built up much goodwill as he did far more than a few free jobs for people who were experiencing dark days.

He was almost forty when he married Mary, another migrant from Scotland who was a decade his junior. It was a solid partnership that produced twin sons, who each had no inclination to become plumbers but had visionary ambitions in other areas of the world of business. Sadly, they both died in a car accident on their way home from church one evening, when a drunken driver hit them head-on as he changed lanes on a bend. Mary could not handle her grief, her boys were the light of her life. She took her own life a few months later.

Their son Charles had never married, but his twin, Robert, had a young pregnant wife, Annie. On that fatal evening, she had at the last minute decided not to go to church because she was not feeling one hundred per cent.

When her daughter was born, Annie called her Mary in honour of her tragic mother-in-law. Annie handled the tragedy well but did not marry again or form any close relationships. She was a one-man woman who secured her future by becoming a highly innovative and successful dressmaker. She believed that her talents were God-given and that it was a sin of negligence not to use them. Her father-in-law, Jamie, held the same basic beliefs, indeed even more so. They were both certain that, at some point in everyone's life, tragedies or failures or both were inevitable. However, to give up on life was unforgiveable.

Annie and Jamie lived in separate homes, but she cared for him with devotion, and he responded likewise as he loved both Annie and little Mary. He was enormously proud of them, and was over the moon when Mary married and produced two splendid grandchildren.

Jamie sold his plumbing business at a handsome price when he reached seventy-five, and the proceeds gave him financial independence for the rest of his days. He then spent the next quarter of a century establishing and leading the Mary Glasgow Mental Health Trust. Clearly, its origins grew in his mind from the time when Mary had taken her own life. He was thunderstruck on that horrible day. Throughout their relationship, she had been such a strong and stable person. When Robert and Charles were killed, he and Mary had sustained one another magnificently, and he was convinced they had worked their way through the tragedy out into the light.

Then, one day, she told him she was going shopping. She did not come back and never would. She had deliberately driven her car over a cliff. No other vehicles had been anywhere in sight, nor was she driving on a difficult section of road. No farewell note was left behind. She said goodbye to no one. After much agony, Jamie came to believe that she had wanted to die in a car accident, as this was the way her beloved sons had been killed, even though the circumstances were different.

For years, Jamie pondered it all. Some years back, he had been elected an Elder of the Presbyterian Church, a position he had declined earlier as he felt he was not a worthy person. He carried out his duties with great dedication and commitment, spending many hours and days and years as a caring leader of the pastoral care team. He loved visiting people who needed a friend.

So it was that when he sold his plumbing business, he decided to devote his remaining years, twenty-five of them as it transpired, to researching mental health and care of mental health sufferers via the Mary Glasgow Mental Health Trust. He was still its president at one hundred years old, and he kept on trying to stop people from taking their own lives at times of grief.

Annie continued to look after him lovingly in his old age, but five years ago he decided that he must never become a burden on her life. Despite her strong protests, he decided to take up residence at The Haven.

It was the greatest mistake of his entire life.

Jamie quickly came to regard The Haven as a prison. Life was heavily regimented, allowing no space for any expression of compassion. The place had a policy of keeping its residents quiet and docile at a minimum cost. The place was kept clean, but there was no effort to give the residents a life. The policy of The Haven was to keep them in basic comfort until they died, while earning as much money from them as they possibly could by charging them for trivial extras.

In between meals, and sometimes for occasional entertainment, the residents looked at walls and were put to bed early with a good sleeping tablet. They were not allowed to express themselves in any way other than by observing a strict routine. The thought that residents may have a capacity to be productive was not even remotely on the radar of management.

Jamie gave them credit for the way they had moved quickly to halt a threatened outbreak of Covid-19, but it was clear that a rebellion was needed, and he decided to lead it. In doing so, he became a significant problem to management. He was determined to keep an active lifestyle, and this meant he wanted his mental health crusade to continue, as his brain was still sharp and he felt that he still had a capacity to lead. It was only his body that was a problem.

So, without asking permission, James held small executive meetings in his room and had limousines come and pick him up to take him to board meetings. The management of The Haven was not impressed. He was giving the other residents 'bad' ideas. Jamie did not deny it. He knew that his activities were encouraging others to do things that were not part of the accepted routine, and so it did not surprise him when management decided to put a stop to it. They banned business meetings in his room. But they could not stop him travelling to board meetings when driven there and back by other people.

Sadly, Jamie's arthritis got progressively worse with every passing year, and he kept growing more and more skin cancers. Even worse, he was having difficulty in swallowing. He gradually came to the conclusion that he had had enough. It was time to step into eternity.

———

Jamie decided to call Graeme Brown and ask if he could drop by for a coffee and a good chat about voluntary assisted dying. He had noted that someone had leaked to the media the news of Graeme's decision regarding VAD.

He had met Graeme on several occasions, and had once invited him to be guest speaker at the annual meeting of the Mary Glasgow Mental Health Trust. Graeme gave a wonderfully inspiring and fascinating address about the growing number of people who found life to be absolutely pointless, and who tried to handle that situation in a wide range of ways, most of them failing badly.

Graeme readily agreed to a meeting. He was an admirer of Jamie and offered to come to The Haven to meet him there. Jamie demurred, asking if he could come to Graeme's residence where he could talk more freely.

'Welcome to my home, Jamie, and congratulations on reaching your century.'

'It's good of you to make time to meet me, Graeme. I want to have a frank talk with you about voluntary assisted dying.'

'Are you about to tell me that you have joined the ranks of those like me who have a terminal illness?'

'No, I have just had enough of life on earth and I want to move on.'

'What has caused you to want to move on?'

'Can I give you a long explanation?'

'You may.'

'I was born in Scotland but came here to find a new life. I did well in business, then married Mary, as lovely a partner as any man could wish for. We lost our two sons in the same car accident, and then, not all that long afterwards, Mary took her own life. It all happened in the same year, but I steadily recovered with the aid of Annie, the wife of one of the sons I lost. We have lived separate but close lives. Annie is a very loving human being.

When I got to seventy-five, I sold my plumbing business at a good price and settled down to create and lead a mental health trust in honour of Mary, whose mental illness led to her suicide. That trust has done good things to help those who are stricken as Mary was.'

'It certainly has, Jamie. You are a splendid community servant who has given superb leadership to the trust, a good role model for others to follow in community service.'

'I do feel good about what the trust has achieved, Graeme, and I have been able to build a great team around me who will carry it on in my absence.'

'Exactly why do you want to be absent, Jamie? You are still as bright as a button.'

'I want to meet Mary again and do it soon.'

'Tell me what your plan is.'

'My Christian faith is very simple, Graeme, unlike yours. I have read all your books and enjoyed them. I greatly respect your sincerity, but your faith and mine have always been on a different pathway. I am an old-fashioned Presbyterian who believes that God created me and my destiny and helped me achieve it. I have faithfully served his Church and tried to live a life of personal decency and service to humanity. I strongly believe in life after death. I have not the slightest doubt about it, but I know that you don't share my view on that.

Mary's suicide shocked our church, but not me. It wounded me deeply, but I loved her and still do. I know that she would never let me or our God down. She had a reason for taking her own life, and I want to talk with her about it. I reckon I will find her if I die by my own actions, just like she did. I want to use voluntary assisted dying, but I can't do it here as I am not terminally ill. I am just old and in a state of steady decline. I will have to go to Switzerland. My actions will be legal there.'

Graeme's response was instant. 'Jamie, you should go there and go soon. You may have travel problems due to Covid-19, but there must be a way to overcome that.'

'There is. Travel only becomes a problem if I try to come back, and I am not coming back. In Switzerland, I will self-isolate by dying.'

'Have you made contact with a hospital in Switzerland?'

'Not yet. I wanted to talk to you first to assure myself that I am doing the right thing. You and I are on the same path, but for different reasons.'

'You are doing the right thing and I want to help. I have a friend in Switzerland who is an eminent doctor. From time to time, he helps people to voluntarily die. It is not his full-time area of practicing medicine, but he is ready to help when called upon by people he knows and respects. I can call him to arrange everything for you, if this is your wish.'

'It is.'

'Right, you can give me the personal details I need and we can go to work immediately.'

'Can I ask you something? You don't believe in life after death, so why are you helping me when your belief is that Mary and I will not meet again?'

'I am involved because you are my friend and you honoured me by seeking my help. If it is even remotely possible for you to meet Mary, I want to help you achieve this. Like you, I have not experienced death. Thus my personal belief that there is no life after death is just a firmly held conviction. However, it is not an indisputable fact because I have not yet died and proved my conviction of its non-existence. I want to help you to find out, as it is a very important matter in your life. I hope that you prove me wrong and find Mary.'

'It was a great day when I first met you, Graeme Brown. I am certain that my God directed me to you.'

'If he did, it was one of his better days and we have both benefitted.'

Graeme then brewed his finest coffee and shared it with Jamie. They chatted about their families and gave thanks that they had been blessed with the very finest. As they departed, Jamie stood at the door and watched the autumn leaves falling.

'Autumn is a lovely season and evenings are my happiest hours,' he said. 'You and I are doing something special. We are sharing our last autumn and treasuring our final evenings in peace with God.'

'We are. Bless you, Jamie.'

Chapter Seven

Aisha greeted Graeme warmly. They had always had a good and open relationship in which they shared mutual trust. He had come to her surgery for one of their regular reviews of his medical condition, even though it was, in reality, rather pointless. His health was in a state of steady decline and he was losing weight, but his eyes were bright and revealed no evidence of pain. And his attitude was resolutely positive, as usual. He was moving steadily and purposefully along a carefully planned route to the end of his life at a specific time and place, an occurrence that few people would experience with certainty.

After a review of recent reports from specialist radiologists and physicians and a thorough examination of his general condition, Aisha gave him some interesting suggestions about changes to his diet that would aid his retention of vigour, as well as some new prescriptions for slightly stronger medication, with an assurance that it would not impede his ability to live actively and to keep kicking some important goals.

Aisha asked him how Penelope was handing the situation.

'Like the champion she is,' Graeme replied, 'always has been and always will be.'

'I am delighted to hear that.'

'Have you got some time to listen to what happened?'

'Yes. I anticipated that you might want to talk for a little longer today, so I have delayed my next appointment.'

'Thanks for that. Here is what happened. I walked home on the day you gave me my fatal news. Left my car right here in your carpark. Fortunately for me, Luke and Fiona came to pick it up later. I then walked around the park and sat under a large and shady old tree to meditate and make plans. That quiet hour got me prepared, so I walked on home and conveyed your findings to Penelope immediately without playing around with words. She was incredible. She stared lovingly at me for a few moments, then walked into my arms and hugged me tightly for a long time without saying a word. Then she whispered, 'I will walk with you every step of the way.' I replied, 'I will love you every step of the way.'

She led me to our bedroom, and we made love slowly and tenderly in the hope that it would never end. We said not a word. Silence was golden. In all of our passionate years together, this was the most magnificent hour. Finally, we fell asleep. I had never before experienced such peace. I hoped that Penelope felt likewise.

When I woke an hour later, she was not beside me. I walked around our home wondering where she was. I found her out in the garden all set up under a tree with two chairs and a small table, together with two glasses, a small container of ice, and a new bottle of one of my favourite single malt scotch whiskies, Highland Park from the Orkney Islands. She had deliberately selected a whisky from the Scottish Islands as they are remote and alone and peaceful, as we were at that moment. But it also reminded us that we were drinking on the very frontier of life.

Penelope said to me, 'Come here and sit down. We have a lot of somewhat urgent business to chat about.' We have been talking ever since. But before we actually got down to business on that memorable day, she said, 'Remember the day we first met? You preached your first sermon at my church and our eyes connected. Then when we shook hands at the door, our eyes connected a bit longer than they should have. Later you told me that when you first noticed me during the sermon, you said to yourself, "That's her." Can I say how wonderful it has been to have been chosen as her?'

I can now tell you, Aisha, that my response when I saw her in church that day was actually electric. I paused to take another quick look. The congregation thought that I was deliberately pausing to build up expectation for a dramatic comment. I did make one, just to impress this lovely girl. That sermon became special for both Penelope and me. I never preached it again. I had called it the "Impossible Dream", and it was about Moses' dream that he would lead his people out of bondage in Egypt and take them to a new land that flowed with milk and honey. For Penelope and me, our life together came to be the achievement of the impossible dream. We have had endless experiences that have tasted better than all the finest milk and honey in the world.

So, Aisha, the milk and honey has not stopped flowing despite the arrival of cancer. We are ready. Both of us. Importantly, there is no fear in our souls. I am ready for death, and Penelope is ready to live without me.'

'This is splendid. How did Fiona and Luke respond?'

'They were magnificent too. With tears in their eyes, they asked lots of questions about how I was planning to handle life in my final days, and they then wanted to form a partnership with Penelope and me as we walked along an avenue that all four of us knew would come to an abrupt but peaceful end.'

As the consultation proceeded, Aisha and Graeme discussed his mental health. She was concerned that even though the initial reaction of his family had been both mature and calm, problems could arise. Graeme said that he was confident that he was in good shape. He and Penelope had been initially concerned that Luke and Fiona might be quietly grieving while still putting on a positive front, but they seemed to be travelling well. Initially they were stunned, but he was amazed at how quickly they had come to terms with his death, and their regular family chats about it had indicated how well they had come to accept the reality of it all. He was convinced that they were not in a silent state of grief. But even if they were, he knew that grief was another form of expressing love.

The entire family realised that, as they had only three months left, there was only one pathway forward. They should all do their best to enjoy it. Weeping and wailing and anger were pointless. And so it had been. They were doing wonderful things together.

A major hurdle was to mutually accept and finally agree that voluntary assisted dying was the way to go. Fiona did not want him to go one moment earlier than he absolutely had to, but she was even more determined to ensure that he should not suffer. Luke needed to convince himself that VAD was not suicide. He worked his way through that, finally determining that Graeme, already close to death, was merely determining what was the best timing for the inevitable to occur.

They both thought that it was splendid that a tree would grow in the national park as a symbol of his life. It would be ever so much better than a cold tombstone and would be a symbol that death was all about life.

Importantly, too, they quickly agreed on how his estate should be distributed. It was not a trivial matter, as the royalties from Graeme's books were considerable, meaning that they would be financially independent for the remainder of their lives as long as they invested their capital conservatively and wisely.

Penelope was insistent that Luke and Fiona should not have to wait until her death to get their share of the family assets. So it was agreed that each will receive one quarter immediately. The remaining quarter would be put into a charitable trust for which all three of them would be the only trustees. They unanimously decided that all of its income would be used to protect and enhance the environment, a cause that they believed Jesus of Nazareth would approve of.

Aisha and Graeme talked about the progress of his application to leave the world via voluntary assisted dying. So far there seemed to be no insurmountable hurdles to overcome in ending his life on his own terms.

As the safeguards for VAD were comprehensive and prolonged, she again asked him if it was still his intention to proceed by VAD. On receiving his firm affirmative response, she asked him to sign yet another document that recorded this decision. This was an unavoidable requirement of the law. He would sign yet more forms, even on the day of his death. There could be no misunderstandings.

Graeme had already been interviewed and examined by three medical specialists independent of Aisha, as well as having met separately with two psychiatrists and a government representative. All had now affirmed in writing that he was terminally ill but sound of mind, fully able to understand the total finality of the steps he was determined to take.

They fixed the date and the precise time and arranged a booking at the hospital. For all intents and purposes, Graeme had a precise number of days to live. He intended to use them as well as he was able. He would not sit around waiting to die. He would share many happy days with family and friends, as well as contribute to the life of anyone who asked for his advice and help.

At this point, he was unaware that four people would call on his goodwill to humanity.

———

Graeme and Aisha's positive chat moved on as he gave her an outline of how he had occupied his time beyond his family since they had last met, and what unfinished business he now planned to undertake.

He was able to report to her on his delightful encounter with the local funeral director.

Wanting to be in charge of all aspects of his departure, he had called the local funeral parlour to tell the owner that he wanted to select his own coffin and chat about funeral arrangements, as he planned that his departure would be different to most. He asked if he could come at 5pm that day, having chosen this time because he wanted to share a top-quality whisky with him while they chatted about all the finer points of his funeral. The guy readily accepted this with obvious enthusiasm. Who wouldn't be happy? A whisky with one of the world's most famous authors was something to look forward to. In Graeme's mind, he would always think of him by the happy name of Funeral Pal.

He went to his whisky cupboard and selected a Lagavulin, a wee dram that in his view was the ultimate in perfection. It came from a splendid distillery on the Isle of Islay, which is the most southerly of the Western Isles of Scotland where he and Penelope had visited some years back. This island, which is offshore from Glasgow, is actually a huge lump of peat that is a few million years old. When the distillery strains the whisky through the smoke of burning peat, it gives it the most powerful aroma that stays with you for a whole evening—as well as really clearing your brain, nose and throat. Penelope declared it to be ghastly, but she had this view about all whiskies. Her drink of choice was a sauvignon blanc, especially if it came from New Zealand.

Funeral Pal had fine whisky glasses ready. They were crystal. Graeme poured two substantial wee drams and settled down to outline his thoughts about his departure. He became more relaxed with every moment, wondering why so many people avoided going to funeral parlours.

Could Funeral Pal make an elegant-looking coffin from dried seaweed? Graeme did not want his death to cause any more destruction to the depleted forests of the world, and he had read in a magazine that a process had been discovered by which it was possible to turn seaweed into a building material.

Funeral Pal did not bat an eyelid. Yes, this was certainly possible. Funeral Pal knew a guy who specialised in creating seaweed products. He mentioned to Graeme that after all his decades in the funeral business, he could attest with certainty that Graeme was the only one to depart in a seaweed coffin. Funeral Pal took another sip of Lagavulin and, with a broad smile and wink, expressed the view that seaweed would probably burn quicker and brighter than wood.

'Great,' Graeme said. 'Could I have it painted white?'

'Absolutely.'

'Could you create some words in flowers to place on the top of the white seaweed coffin?'

'Yes. What words and what flowers?'

'"Graeme and the Great Spirit are work mates." Done with rose petals. Very red ones.'

Now for the more difficult stuff, thought Graeme. Could Funeral Pal arrange for an oak tree to be planted on a hill in the nearby national park where Graeme's ashes could be put in the hole before the tree was planted? And could he make sure that the chosen plant was of the finest quality, which would one day grow to be a giant oak, preferably higher than any other oak in the forest?

'Yes, no problem at all,' said Funeral Pal. 'What plaque or sign would you like to be placed beside it?'

'None,' Graeme said. His wife and family were the only ones who needed to know where it was located. They will help to plant it and can decide from time to time which of their friends they will take there to say hello to Graeme and to watch it grow.

'Done.'

'Send a quote,' Graeme said. 'Whatever the price may be, I'll pay it well in advance.'

In what church will the funeral be held? Graeme thought. This was outstanding business. It may not be in a church. Details will be decided soon. Graeme did not enjoy a close relationship with churches at this moment. Some repairs and maintenance needed to be carried out by both sides.

There was a pleasant silence while they took another delightful sip of Lagavulin. Then with the business end of their meeting out of the way, Funeral Pal had some thoughts he wanted to express.

'My friend, you are the most fascinating customer who has ever come through my office door, and I fervently hope you are not the last one of your quality.'

'How do I come to have earned this honour?'

'Well, for starters, I do not usually make deals directly with the deceased. They often come here to buy a funeral plan well in advance, but don't turn up to organise all the details beforehand.'

'This is a shame, as they miss out on all the excitement. I have found our chat today to be absolutely refreshing. It has made me feel that I may well enjoy the actual experience.'

'You show no fear of death whatsoever.'

'As death is part of life, the final curtain call in fact, it should be enjoyed if circumstances make this possible.'

'Nevertheless, your calm is almost overpowering.'

'Fact is that I have no option. Five specialists have affirmed that, without any shadow of a doubt, I have terminal cancer and have only a short time left. I do have a choice. I can be frightened, miserable, bitter and whinge about why this is happening to a splendid chap such as myself. Or I can decide to enjoy it all and go out with an encore that makes my family and friends feel happy. Well, I have chosen the latter. It's the best deal by far. I plan that my personal final curtain call will be an absolute cracker, as I can never put on a repeat performance. You are welcome to join me for drinks on the day before I die.'

'That will be an enormous privilege, but tell me, how will you know what day to hold it? Or will your family give me an urgent phone call at a few hours' notice?'

'I will know the exact day and will advise you well in advance. I have done all the legal work necessary to arrange for my life to end via voluntary assisted dying. I am currently having serious discussions with my doctor, Aisha Jinnah, as to what day she feels will be close to the last time I will be well enough to appear at a party and enjoy myself. You will receive an invitation for drinks at 5pm that day, and I will die at 3pm the following day. We will give you precise details shortly.'

'Two questions. At the wake you are holding in advance, how can I possibly work out what to say to a man who has just hours to live? And how will you cope with the enormous pressure created by your need to say lots of final words to your friends, especially when your personal strength could well be rapidly diminishing at that point?'

'You and I will find words, as will everyone else, as we will have no alternative at that time.'

'Well, I can tell you that I am lost for words right now.'

'This being so, it is an opportune time for us to end our pleasant conversation and look forward to the next. Thank you for a relaxing hour and for your willingness to arrange my funeral in the exact way that I hope it will be. It's a pleasure and a privilege to do business with you. It is really sad that I can never be a repeat customer.'

———

Aisha was somewhat at a loss for words herself when Graeme finished his tale. Nevertheless, she took another deep breath and decided that it was time to mention her challenging request to a dying man for his personal help with a person who, like him, had real life and death problems.

But before she could get started on that, Graeme had another story to tell her.

'As I was walking back to my home from the funeral parlour, I crossed paths with our local rabbi, Jacob Isaacs. I have known him quite well for some time and have met him regularly in academic and literary circles where he has made a respected name for himself as a profound writer of books on morality.'

He greeted me warmly.

'Good afternoon, Graeme, have not seen you for a long time. What have you been up too lately?'

'Dying.'

'We are all doing that. Are you dying quicker than the rest of us?'

'Yes.'

'What in particular are you dying from at this moment?'

'Cancer.'

'My friend, I am very sorry to hear this. Now that I take particular notice, you are not looking as well as you usually do.'

'Not really feeling well either.'

'Tell me your story.'

'A group of eminent cancer gurus agreed a few weeks ago that I had terminal cancer. Irrevocably set into five places in my body and growing steadily.'

'Do you have time to have a coffee with me while we chat about this?'

'I do.'

'There is a quaint little place just around the corner. Run by a delightful gay couple who make superb coffee and magnificent whisky shortbread biscuits. Let's drop in there for a while.'

They found a quiet corner at the Rainbow Cafe, and Graeme quietly and peacefully told his story as they sipped their long blacks and nibbled the splendid biscuits.

'The key issue about which I seek your wise counsel, Jacob,' said Graeme, 'is that of my clear and unshakeable decision to end my life soon by voluntary assisted dying. I seek your blunt opinion of the morality of my decision and its religious implications. I believe that my intentions and actions are soundly based, but, obviously, I am not infallible.'

'Firstly, let me say this, Graeme. I am bowled over by the news that cancer will shortly take your life, but I feel strength flowing to me by the peace and the courage with which you so calmly face the end of your life.'

He reached out to firmly grasp Graeme's hand, and said, 'I love you greatly, my brother. Now, let me say these few things. The laws of our land allow voluntary assisted dying, so your death will be a lawful act that will not be recorded as a suicide, and, indeed, it must never be regarded as that.

Some fundamentalist conservatives, religious and political, will declare it to be suicide because that is the limit of their narrow minds, but you can totally ignore them even if your own church attacks you. The issue for you lies far beyond those people and its impact is two-fold. The first is your personal relationship with God, and the second is the morality of what you are doing. If you are happy for me to do so, I am willing to discuss both of these issues with you now while we continue to enjoy this splendid coffee.'

'I greatly welcome this discussion, Jacob. My death from cancer, whether it be the will of God or an act of nature, is now a fact. All that I am doing is bringing it forward by a few weeks to save my family from the agony of watching me slowly fade away. Additionally, I am creating circumstances in which my death is a happy event, not one of sadness. I am doing some good things as a pastor in my final weeks, walking with people who have huge problems. Then, on the evening before my final day, I will host a small gathering for drinks with a few valued friends and family to happily and sincerely say farewell. I hope that you will be able to accept my invitation to attend.'

'Thanks for those comments, and, yes, it will be an honour to attend your final party. I can understand your thinking as you grapple with a very personal situation. Let us then look at your relationship with God. Do you imagine that, at your death, you will have to account to God for your actions?'

'No. I have accounted to God for my actions throughout my life. I do not believe in life after death or the existence of Heaven or Hell. When I am dead, I am dead.'

'Well, Graeme, as you know, my field of academic knowledge is centred on morality, and the longer I live, the longer I study, and the more I get involved in research on human behaviour, the further I am convinced that there will never be a uniform code of morality that is acceptable to everyone or practised by all. It is a personal matter, and personal decisions will often defy logic. For instance, it is a pointless exercise to try to be moral just to please God. We must be our own judge and jury. Our personal morality becomes a cornerstone of our existence, and I believe that your personal cornerstone is solid. I find nothing immoral about what you are doing. Now, what do you hope I might say to you at this moment that will be a comfort to you as you travel through your final days?'

'Your words have strengthened me,' said Graeme. 'I am grateful. Your friendship is important to me.'

'All that I can say is that I am privileged to share your journey. So, as we continue to enjoy this fine coffee, can we have a chat about all of the books you have written? What do you hope that people worldwide will remember from their reading of your books and their application of them to their lives?'

This topic created an animated discussion about the legacy of fine words that Graeme was leaving for the people of the world to use well if they chose to do so. They agreed that as long as people read his books and this changed their lives, his spirit would live on. Rabbi Jacob was certain that Graeme's books were a great legacy that would enhance humanity for a long time to come. Soon it was time to go, and Jacob began to wind up the conversation.

'I am very proud to be of the Jewish faith and tradition. As a race of people, we have been accused of many sins for thousands of years. We have been persecuted for being unclean and of dishonesty in accumulating money. My grandfather escaped the Holocaust in Vichy France—where Pétain was even more vicious than Hitler—only because he had skills in mathematics that the government needed.

The one accusation that has always stuck in my craw as the most offensive is the claim that we betrayed Jesus and were responsible for his crucifixion. That is patently untrue and unfair. Jesus deliberately went to Jerusalem that first Easter to confront his detractors and his enemies. He did not have to go. He could have saved himself by using the right words when hauled in front of his judges. Do you think it is possible that he publicly carried out a very high-profile form of voluntary euthanasia? His death was totally avoidable?'

'I do indeed. I back your interpretation of that momentous event with total conviction. Jesus made a deliberate choice to go to his death.'

'Let me make this parting comment, Graeme. I have been saddened to note that our generation has lost the art of dying well. My hope is that your highly commendable attitude to death will reverse this trend and lead many to happier end of life experiences.'

———

'Would you like to become an active priest again during the last weeks of your life?'

'Why do you ask me that, Aisha?'

'Let me explain a disturbing situation to you, Graeme. I have a difficult patient who is a high-profile member of the Christian Right and is close to death from Covid-19. He can't cope with it, and he needs help coming to terms with the fact that his life is within days of being over. He is obsessed with the possibility that his God may be angry with him for reasons that he cannot understand, as he passionately believes that he has been a good and faithful servant who has done God's work for many years.'

'Give me more details,' said Graeme.

'His name is Scott Palmer.'

'Know of him. He is a big wheel around town, even though he is only around forty years old, but I have never met him face to face. I have listened to some of his high-profile podcasts on the Prosperity Gospel. That unfounded belief switches me off massively, as it is a religious cover for personal greed. Even so, I have no doubt that he passionately believes it.'

'He had been diagnosed with a variant of Covid-19 and is rapidly succumbing to it. It's the worst case that has occurred in our city so far. I doubt that he can last more than a few days even though he was physically quite healthy before he got this virus. The fact is that he is mentally unable to fight it.'

'What do you want me to do?'

'Talk personally with him at his hospital room.'

'How do we achieve this and what outcome do you hope for?'

'Let's deal with the practicalities. Firstly, he must agree to meet you face to face, and it is my task to achieve this. I believe that he will, as I have discussed the possibility with him. Number two is that you will be required to be totally covered with protective gear and to stay no longer than fifteen minutes. His strength will be totally exhausted by then. Your words must come slowly and clearly and be very powerful.'

'What do you want me to talk about?'

'I want you to teach him how to die.'

'You reckon I can do this in fifteen minutes, especially when I obviously have no personal experience of dying? I am sure that you have noted that my time is yet to come.'

'I accept the validity of the problem you raise, but it is absolutely crucial that you make this encounter as productive as possible in these circumstances. He absolutely cannot understand why his God is punishing him. Up until this time in his life, he has believed that he had a particularly close relationship with God. Indeed, he was certain that he held the highest possible ranking in the spiritual pecking order as anyone could possibly achieve. He should not die in this shattered state of faith and in fear of God.'

'Will he listen to me?'

'I think so. I have advised him that it is important that he does, and, even though he is confused, his response seems to be positive. He knows that you have only weeks to live and are at peace. He is amazed at this and has serious questions about how you achieved this extraordinary state of mind when you belong to the Christian Left. He has always believed that people on the left have a very shallow faith.'

'When do you hope that I can do this?'

'Tomorrow. The day after may be too late. If you can manage 7am that will be wonderful. This fits in with my hospital round and the timing of his intensive treatment. Both he and the medical team insist that I be present to ensure that he is not pushed beyond his physical and spiritual capacity.

Apparently, he gains confidence when I am with him. He regards me as his guardian angel, even though he sacked me when I told him that he had Covid-19.'

'What caused you to be reinstated?'

'His wife, Pauline, reversed his decision. She is a fundamentalist Christian, but not 'happy clappy' like him. Oddly, she is apparently a defender of human rights, especially for women, a strange occupation for a fundamentalist.'

'An interesting combination of beliefs.'

'Yes, it is. Let me once more affirm that I must constantly monitor his ability to continue to participate in the conversation once it gets under way, and I will act instantly if it should be necessary. He must not die as the result of any stress caused by talking with you.'

'Okay. Count me in. With only twenty-four hours to prepare myself for this task, I will need to be at my best, otherwise this will be a total waste of time for all of us, as well as an awful human tragedy.'

'I have another important question for you. Are you well enough to handle this? Do you have the energy, both mentally and physically, to do this? You are steadily losing weight and you are starting to look a little weary.'

'I can handle it. In reality, it gives me yet another opportunity to live positively throughout my final days. It also makes me feel useful. I am not a dead weight in the saddle bags of humanity.'

———

Graeme decided to share the Palmer challenge with his family at dinner that evening. This created no problems for Penelope, Fiona and Luke, as they became fascinated by the task when Graeme came home to tell them about it. It was another stark reminder of the issues involved for them in coming to terms with life and death as each day passed.

Graeme set the framework of the debate by asking some questions.

'Can we talk firstly about the man, Scott Palmer. What sort of person is he? Do we really understand enough about his faith and his attitude to money and destiny?'

'From time to time,' said Fiona, 'I have read some opinion pieces about him in the media. It seems that he is genuinely a 'born again Christian' who gradually became a happy clappy but who does not speak in tongues or pretend to perform miracles. Apparently, he is quite conservative in all his habits and is very serious about his personal faith. In fact, he does not seem to be an exhibitionist in any way, even though he has a high profile as a promoter of Christian causes. So I can understand why he will be upset if he thinks he has become offside with God. He may well be reluctant to confide his inner thoughts to you, Graeme.'

Luke had other ideas. 'I am very switched off by his belief in and his practice of the Prosperity Gospel. It is one of the greatest lies ever told to the human race. I just don't believe we can or should use our faith as the cornerstone from which we can make money. If, as Christians, our faith happens to give us a positive edge in making a good living because we are doing good work, then that is a different matter, but it must never be the prime purpose of any work. As you know, Graeme, I have some friends who are devout Christians and who work in ordinary jobs earning low pay, but they are happy with their lives and find purpose in their community service.'

Penelope had critical thoughts about Scott's belief that all his actions are the will of God, his destiny in fact. 'It all sounds like a fairy tale. He seems to be the equivalent of a Christian robot.'

Graeme acknowledged the validity of their comments and added some further thoughts. 'I am concerned that Scott could have had such belief in his destiny that he is certain that God would exempt him and his fellow believers from Covid-19 and every other hazard that crossed their paths. It is both naïve and selfish. Added to this, he has believed that God would also protect him from any business problems that may stop him from achieving the goals throughout his calling as a Christian. He has been living in his dreamworld, and now it has begun to come apart at a time when he can do little about it.'

Penelope asked if a dying man could really have an in-depth talk with anyone about any matters that are deep in the core of his faith, especially with another person who faced the same issue. However, she suggested, perhaps Graeme's situation may create a bond between them that bridges their clear theological gap. Both Luke and Fiona were concerned that this difficult encounter would test Graeme's physical and mental strength to the limit of his endurance.

'I think I can handle it, so long as I remain utterly calm throughout our talk and do my best to keep him calm. As Aisha suggested, I must discover ways of talking very simply but powerfully.'

'What in the simplest possible terms is the main point you will make to him?' asked Fiona.

'I may change my mind overnight, but my current thinking is that he should simply convey to his God that he is still his servant, even though he is now unsure as to what God's will is.'

Graeme looked very tired. They suggested that he get to bed and sleep quickly, as they were all certain that this action would be God's will for him at this precise moment.

He did as they had suggested. But weary though he was, it took some minutes for sleep to come to him. He pondered the fact that on the next morning two men who sat on the edge of eternity would discuss why they were there. Perhaps there could be hope that they would find some common ground. After all, a basic and precious element of Christianity is hope.

Chapter Eight

Graeme could barely hear Scott's voice. It was minutely above a whisper. He had discussed this possibility with Fiona as she drove him to the hospital half an hour ago.

'You may have a big problem this morning, Graeme, when you sit beside Scott Palmer's bed to try to talk with him. He may be too ill to get many words out, and you may have no option but to speak loudly and slowly if he is to hear you.'

'I guess that I will just have to play this by ear when I am with Aisha in his room. As you suggested yesterday, it could be that we may have to call it off abruptly. I will be disappointed if we have to do this, as I have come to feel that this may be a valuable spiritual experience for both Scott and me. I still have a lot to learn about dying myself. I hope that we can share something that is quite unusual.'

'You have now got me really intrigued,' she said as she temporarily parked near the kerb outside the hospital. 'Let me know when to come by to drive you home. It will be a privilege. I am enormously proud to be your daughter.'

'Thanks. It will be good to do a critical review of it as we drive along. You are a lovely daughter and also a wise one whose opinions I greatly respect.'

Now he was seated in the tightly sealed atmosphere of the isolation ward that shielded Scott from the rest of humanity. His chair had been placed against a wall so as to have the maximum physical distance from Scott, and he was covered from head to toe in protective gear. He looked like Neil Armstrong as he prepared to step out onto the moon. The situation seemed to be quite unreal. Scott appeared to be in another world. Securely apart from him was a tent that seemed substantial enough to stop a bullet, and he was connected to every possible medical device and computer that even the greatest science fiction writer could not have possibly imagined.

Nevertheless, they could see one another clearly, and they were connected by tiny sophisticated phones built into their protection gear that were able to be easily amplified or softened according to the needs of the situation.

Graeme again marvelled at the fact that this was actually happening after much discussion between Aisha and Scott. Astonishingly, Scott had this morning responded positively to Aisha's announcement that Graeme was outside ready to meet him if he was willing to go ahead. The stage had been set, with Aisha having briefed them both on their different personal and religious backgrounds. The ventilator had been temporarily removed from Scott's face for fifteen minutes. Their conversation would finish completely at that time, otherwise his life could be in real danger.

'Hello, Scott. My name is Graeme, and one month from now I will be dead. I have terminal cancer, and several of the best cancer specialists in our city have studied my case and they can do nothing for me. My only future in this world is death, so I have chosen to end my life by undergoing a medical process called voluntary assisted dying. It will not be the prime cause of my death. It will just enable me to die at an earlier date as the result of my acceptance of the inevitable. I am doing it primarily to ensure that my wife and children do not have to watch me waste away to a ghastly end of life.'

The response from Scott was slow and clearly energy sapping. 'Only God decides when we die. Strongly disagree with your decision. Insult to Almighty.'

'Scott, God has already decided that I will die and will do so very soon. I have simply brought forward whatever date he had in mind. I am in no conflict with Him.'

Scott struggled to breathe. He went on, gasping, 'Still disagree, but value your time with me. It's precious to you and your family.'

'I am pleased to be able to give the time, as I know that you still have a chance to live. I have no hope, but you have.'

With an increasing struggle, Scott continued, 'Doctors very blunt. Told them to spare no expense. I can pay. They say I do not respond to treatment or medication they give me. Don't know what to do next. My life fading away. Will be dead before you are.'

'I hope that you do not believe that God caused you to get this virus that may kill you, and, therefore, that this means He is punishing you for reasons you cannot understand. You are wrong if you do, as you have clearly been a good, faithful and creative servant for many years.'

Aisha interrupted to put Scott back on the ventilator, as he appeared to be near exhaustion. After what seemed a long while, he indicated that he was ready to continue.

'God has led me through life,' Scott said. 'Achieved nothing without Him. Led me to marvellous project that will reform way Christians do business. Now seems it is not his will. Blocking me. Can't understand why.'

Graeme decided it was now time to take a risk. He would make a comment that may well upset Scott, but time was short and there were things that could not be left unsaid.

'Without in any way meaning to cause offence to you personally, can I say with absolute conviction that God has not stopped you from doing anything? Without deliberately setting out to do so, you separated yourself from Him. You were wrong to join with many other reckless people at your church who defy basic common sense and who continue with mass meetings and regular worship in spite of Covid-19 restrictions. This has caused many people to die and many more to become ill. You are an intelligent man and your close relationship with God should have told you that this was stupid behaviour that could even be regarded as an act of murder. Jesus of Nazareth would never have acted so irresponsibly. You cannot blame God for what you did. You brought this all on yourself. God is not punishing you. You punished yourself.'

'Deep trust in God made us believe that He would always protect us.'

'God does nothing of the sort, Scott. What you did has been a huge abuse of your faith in God. He could not protect you when you knowingly and irresponsibly walked headlong into a disease that has the power to kill you and your friends. You must stop blaming Him for forsaking you and take the full blame yourself. A significant change of attitude right now will greatly help your recovery from this vicious virus and will restore your relationship with God. At this very moment, you are destroying yourself. Can you accept your mistake with this immediately? You may have little time left to make this vital spiritual decision.'

Graeme was aware that he sounded like an old-time fundamentalist preacher calling for repentance, but this was language that this man was used to hearing throughout his religious life. Scott was still struggling to come to terms with the interruption to his previously clear journey of faith.

'Your words have torn my faith apart,' said Scott.

'You did that all by yourself, Scott, long before you agreed to meet me.'

'How can I face death in such turmoil within my shattered soul?'

'You can and you will. You and I are facing death in exactly the same way. We can both pass into eternity without fear and with complete faith and trust in God. The decision is solely ours.'

'Grateful for your advice. Am exhausted. Will you pray with me before you go?'

'This will be an honour. But may I first ask you a final question?'

'Yes.'

'Can I have your permission to talk with Pauline about how she can use your personal fortune in a way that will provide new opportunities for Christians who are in real need of a new start in life? It will mean that if you die now you shall continue to work here in this world for Jesus of Nazareth for many years after you have passed on.'

There was total silence. Scott seemed to relax slightly. He seemed to breathe easier. There was a slight hint of renewed life in him as he responded.

'Yes, please.'

'I commit myself to this task on your behalf and will do my utmost to make it happen. Rest in peace.'

'Thank you for the wisdom you have given me. Have listened. Now we have simple plan that is good.'

'May I say, Scott, that my meeting with you here today has helped me come to terms with the journey of my own soul. Let me give a brief prayer, and then you close your eyes and rest. I will leave quietly while Aisha ensures that you can breathe well and that all your medication is working.'

> 'Father, my new friend Scott and I are at a very crucial and challenging time in our lives. Give us the strength of your Spirit to help us to continue on our pathway towards the unknown. We both seek to serve humanity now and after we have gone. May our efforts help to spread the faith in every possible way. Amen.'

Graeme left the room quietly, giving a happy wave to Scott as he walked as close to the bed as he could. Scott lifted has arm slowly and purposefully. Aisha did her work. It seemed to take a long time.

After, she joined Graeme outside and enquired as to how he felt it went.

'I had real misgivings about what had been achieved,' Graeme said, 'until the last few words when we talked about putting his money to work after he has gone. He really did warm to that vision, but his spiritual confusion, combined with his fear of death, is killing him quicker than the virus. Our discussion may have given him a few more moments of life, but the undeniable fact is that he is desperately ill and is not fighting back.

My gut feeling and my only hope is that he may now make a huge resolve to die in peace.'

'So we may not have wasted our time and his.'

'No, I don't think that we did. I hold the firm view that he now accepts that God is not punishing Him and that he alone is responsible for his current state of health.'

'Well, my delay in coming out was caused by him asking me to get his phone from his business case, so that I could send a text message on his behalf to Pauline. He asked her to meet with you about his money. He then made sure she would understand the absolute importance of all this by asking me to send a second message to her on Viber, which said that the first message was vitally important and that she should take it seriously.'

'This is good news. I think it has made my visit worthwhile. I have no doubt that he will die very soon, because he does not want to live in a world that may not fulfill his dreams. After his funeral, we will visit Pauline. I hope that she will agree to meet us.'

'Can we do anything more for Scott?'

'Yes, you can, Aisha. When his time comes, do your utmost to help him die without any more fear.'

'I can only do my best, and I will.'

'Tonight, as I lie in my bed, I will send peaceful thoughts to Scott. Most Christians will call my thoughts a prayer. I call it a chain of peace through which the Great Spirit connects us.'

———

Graeme felt numb. His short time with Scott had drained him emotionally, but he was relatively calm. Fiona drove him home so he could sleep for a couple of hours.

On the way, he said to her, 'I will play a round of golf in the twilight this evening.'

'Who can you line up at short notice to play a round of golf with you?' said Fiona.

'No one. I will play alone.'

'Don't do that. I will walk around with you to keep you company.'

'Thank you, but no. I yearn for a couple of hours of solitude.'

'Let me drive you there and pick you up later.'

'Thanks again, but I will get a cab both ways.'

'Why are you doing this?'

'Solitude.'

'Can you describe what you mean by solitude?'

'Solitude means many things to many people. It is a very individual matter in my case today. It means being out in the open air at a lovely golf course strolling among the trees and the flowers and the lakes and the birds and the bees.'

'Why seek solitude today?'

'I just tried to help a man die, and I would like to think about it in peace.'

'Good idea.'

After Graeme had rested, he phoned the golf club and arranged a tee-off time that would be the last one for the day. Then he booked a cab. He spent the intervening hour answering some of the many emails he was receiving every day from friends, many of whom he had not heard from in years. He enjoyed communicating with them, but he was getting a little slower at opening them every day, and he seemed to be making more typos than usual.

The cab arrived on time, so he set off happily. He had booked only nine holes and had rented a golf cart, but at the last minute he decided to walk even though he knew it would test him to his absolute limit, physically and mentally, as, after allowing for wayward shots, it would mean a walk of about five kilometres. Nevertheless, he believed that he could handle this if he walked slowly and did not get upset when he played lousy shots. So he set off. It was a lovely twilight and peace did surround him.

His drive on the first hole was long but wayward, landing among a cluster of trees. He found the ball okay and decided he could hit it back onto the fairway without having to drop out for a penalty shot. As he stood there wondering about solitude, he remembered reading that trees communicate with one another in various ways. He realised that even in the forests you could not totally achieve solitude, as the trees and bushes and grasses were all chattering.

His shot back onto the fairway had a very narrow pathway. The sensible thing to do was to hit a gentle chip into open spaces. Then he thought, 'I only have a few weeks to live so there is no point in being conservative. Go for glory.'

He lined up carefully and then gave it everything he had. The ball soared beautifully through the gap and a long way down towards the hole.

He yelled with delight. Then chastised himself. 'That is not solitude.'

He played on. Players on other fairways would call out hello, and he would respond happily. He began to forget that he sought solitude. Then it occurred to him that living alone or staying away from crowds did not achieve solitude. It was a self-inflicted isolation. Solitude could only be achieved if you were at peace in big crowds. Why would he ever want to live alone? He knew then that he actually achieved solitude with Fiona and Luke and Penelope because he was at peace in their presence.

On one hole, he missed a short putt of a few centimetres and looked to the heavens asking why. Then another huge truth dawned upon him. In the game of golf, a very short putt is scored the same as a 300-metre drive. Then another thought struck him. In his life, he had spent too much time worrying about trivia and not enough time solving the issues that really mattered.

Finally, he made it back to the clubhouse long after all the players who had been ahead of him. Only just. He felt physically wrecked, but in a state of passable solitude. He wondered if Scott Palmer was experiencing any peace. He hoped so.

The club manager was waiting for him at the edge of the last green. He had realised that he had a VIP on the course, and had read the media reports of Graeme's illness.

'Mr Brown,' the club manager said, 'would you care to join me for a scotch in the peace and quiet of our boardroom? You look a little worn out and need a reviver. I have an old bottle of Port Ellen whisky from the Isle of Islay. The distillery was closed down years ago, but they left a few old barrels behind. I fluked getting of a bottle of it. Its alcohol content is sixty per cent. You only need one nip of it, and you will need to sip it slowly.'

'Sounds splendid,' Graeme said. 'Thank you very much.'

'It's a privilege. Follow me.'

Graeme did sip it slowly, and he ascended into a state of gentle contentment as he chatted with the manager about the fact that golf is a character-building sport. Finally, he asked if the manager would call him a cab.

'No, I will not do that. I will call a limousine and the club will pick up the tab.'

Graeme relaxed in the soft leather seat of the limo and dropped off to sleep in solitude. At least it was his version of solitude at that moment.

Chapter Nine

Jessie heard a knock on the door of her quaint little cottage, tucked away in a quiet suburban street. It was an old timber home on a small block of land, with a cared-for rose garden and some small trees in the back yard where she could hide away. She was delighted that she had been able to rent it at a moderate rate.

She opened the door a little and saw a quite pale woman on her doorstep. She appeared to be most unhappy but was obviously seeking entry. It took Jessie a moment to recognise who it was, particularly as the woman looked so sad and had been previously obscured in the dark.

Can't be anyone else but the park lady, Julia Hawke.

'Come in Julia,' said Jessie.

She had guessed right. Julia did come in.

'Follow me and sit with me on my quiet little leafy terrace out there through the rear door.'

Once settled comfortably, Jessie took the lead, looking a bit uncomfortable as she did so because her guest was a mystery to her.

'We meet in very different circumstances.'

'We do,' said Julia. 'I just wanted to thank you for saving my life.'

'I am not sure that your life really was in danger. You missed the crucial arteries. All I did was organise an ambulance to get you to a hospital where they could sort out the damage you had done to yourself.'

'I am grateful that you did this for me. I cannot thank you enough.'

'I deserve no thanks. I happened to be passing by and did what any other responsible person would have done. Would you mind if I ask you some very direct questions?'

'After the care that you gave me, it would be ungrateful of me not to allow your request.'

'Why did you slash your wrists?'

'My life has been a disaster for a long time. I had reached the point where there was no real reason to stay alive. I simply wanted out.'

'Why was your life not worth living?'

'It has been just awful from the beginning. I was what they call a problem child. I was alienated from my parents, and I was a failure at school. I had difficulty getting any kind of work after I left school, and I could never sustain any kind of relationship, no matter whether it was with a male or female or at work or play. I became pregnant. It could have been any one of three fathers. All of them disappeared. I brought up my daughter alone. But just like I did to my parents in my school days, my daughter left me. Then I finally acknowledged to myself that I was lesbian, and I entered into a same-sex relationship. It was a tragedy too. After a short while, she also left me. That quickly led to the incident that you witnessed in the park.'

'Well, that is a tough life story, but plenty of others have had a much harder time than that. I think you may have given yourself too many doses of self-pity. Be this as it may, while we are being honest with one another, let me tell you my tale of woe. We are not all that dissimilar. We can compare notes.'

'This surprises me. You look like a very nice and respectable little old lady.'

'Looks are deceiving. I am not. I was a dud at school too. Not because of any rebellion but simply because I was not a good student. Matters academic were simply not my scene, then or now.'

'You don't look dumb to me.'

'I must admit that I was a bit dumber at that time than I am now, but the truth is that I graduated with honours from the university of hard knocks. As a matter of fact, I reckon that I earned a doctorate several times over. I learned about life in the raw along every step of the way. I finally realised that if I didn't get a few smart things into my thick head and get myself organised, I was going to wind up on the scrap heap forever. I decided that I would survive by learning to thrive on all the bad things that happened to me.'

'I have never had enough confidence to thrive on anything, good or bad.'

Jessie decided that some blunt words would create an opportunity to open up Julia's world. 'Please don't expect me to feel sorry for you about that. You have probably brought this on yourself. One of the worst diseases in the world is called 'poor little me'. Far too many people get it. If I had known you were suffering from it, I would have left you to die in the park, because self-interest is a very difficult disease to cure.'

'Perhaps you should have. But tell me this, how do I get the confidence that you have?'

'I don't have confidence. I am just immune to fear. If you want confidence, you must get it all by yourself. No one can give it to you, and you can't buy it. All that I did, when it dawned on me that I was a walking problem-generator, was to say to myself, "I must be a human being, otherwise I would not be here. As a human being, I have lots of basic rights. I am going to use them to claw my way up the ladder of life." So I did, and I made lots of mistakes along the way. Took some big hits socially and mentally and financially from time to time, but I made it to where I am now and none of it hurt me permanently.'

'Wow. I don't know if I have the guts to do that.'

'Well, you had better get the guts or you will wind up slashing your wrists in another park on another night.'

'You are making it hard for me. Tell me what actually happened in your life. I need some background that I can latch on to give myself a foothold.'

'It was all quite simple really. I was so unskilled and poorly educated that I could only get the most menial, low-paid cleaning and lawn-mowing jobs. I was saved when a nice guy, who turned out to be more useless than me, asked me to marry him. I thought, "Why not? What have I got to lose by accepting?" So I did, but I soon discovered that he liked booze more than me, and that he had never heard of a condom. Six kids later, I parted company with him on reasonably happy terms, and had a long and tough job getting my kids launched in life. But we made it together as a real team. They are great kids, and all of them helped enormously by getting odd jobs to earn enough money to keep us going. Now they are adults and have all left home and doing okay in jobs of a higher quality than I ever managed to get. I am good friends with all of them, and I dote on the fifteen grandchildren they have given me. They seem to like me too.'

'How old are you now?'

'Eighty-nine.'

'Goodness me. That's an enormous achievement to survive that long after a life lived in such terribly difficult circumstances. Are you okay financially?'

'Before I answer that question, can I say this? If you want to live a long time, then it's vital to work and never retire. It's the guys who stop working early to play golf, go fishing and to have long holidays who die early. I reckon they are a dead loss to the nation. Now, my finances. I survive quite well. I get a government age pension, and this rented house that I have lived in for years is partially covered by a government rent subsidy. I also earn extra money by doing casual work for a few hours here and there. And I have regular holidays visiting my children who seem to be happy for me to come and spend time with them. Can't complain.'

'What hobbies or special interests have you got to keep you occupied when you are not doing casual work?'

'I am the local Miss Marple, you know, the one in the Agatha Christie books who sticks her nose into lots of matters that are none of her business. I quietly find out who is in any sort of trouble around here and I drop round to offer to help. Some rudely tell me to get lost, but most are happy to talk and get advice. I don't have much money to give them, but I go out of my way to find people who can help them. Oh, I am also a champion maker of American pecan pies. I hand them out to people who haven't eaten for a while. Most of them invite me to come back with some more.'

'I am going to have to muster huge amounts of courage to just to get started on a life pathway that is something like yours.'

'You must not copy my life. You must discover your own path. The first steps are the hardest. It gets easier with every subsequent step you take. Let me ask you a question before we work out how you may be able to get yourself relaunched. The background details that Aisha gave me about you indicate that you are an atheist. Why did you choose this path?'

'I have rarely been to any church except for a few weddings and funerals. God has not helped me even once, nor has any Christian ever cared for me. Why should I give God one moment's thought? Christianity is a total fraud, practiced by bigots. Are you a Christian?'

'No, but for very different reasons to yours. I have never been to church, not even for things like weddings and funerals. I deliberately avoid them, and I have never deliberately enquired as to what they teach. I have had to battle for survival every inch of the way all by myself. I did not reckon Christians could help me or would even want to. They are preoccupied with saving their own souls, so I have never contacted them. I don't need any invisible spirit to rev me up.'

'So why did you enquire about my atheism?'

'Well, we all need to believe in something, some sort of goal to aim for, some type of cornerstone in our lives, and I am wondering if you have one. I do. It's not religion and it's not politics. It's music, real old-time music, which has as its theme the struggle of people to survive. Songs like 'This Nearly Was Mine', which was sung by the lonely Frenchman in that wonderful musical *South Pacific*, or like Judy Garland singing 'Somewhere Over the Rainbow.' They gave me hope that there was a better world than that which I experienced, but definitely not the Heaven that dumb Christians reckon they are going to. I will always remember Vera Lynn singing 'We'll Meet Again' to soldiers who were going off to die during World War II. It gave me real hope that there was always another day.'

'I don't have an immediate answer to all that, but you have given me a real challenge to find and work on some sort of motivational foundation for my life. It would be a significant change from having no desire to live at all. I still have in my soul a dark thought that it is all hopeless. I will have to work relentlessly on getting this out of my system.'

'Can I say something that is not intended to hurt you but may do so, because it needs to be said?'

'I am used to feeling hurt, so go ahead.'

'I don't think you really wanted to die when you slashed your wrists in the park. You tried to get public attention to your plight. You deliberately waited for someone to walk through the park, then you cut your wrists, making sure you did not cut your vital arteries, and then you called out. I just happened to be the one who walked by and heard your cry.'

Julia lost her cool, substantially, 'I did not!' she yelled at Jessie. 'I am leaving right at this moment. I will not put up with any insults from an old gossip like you, especially when they are blatant lies.'

She looked at the small vase of flowers sitting on the table and thought seriously about throwing it at Jessie's tiny countenance, but she refrained. She chose instead to pick up her bag and run to the door. She would leave Jessie forever. But before she could get there, Jessie took over once more.

'I will not tolerate screaming from you or have you insult me by walking out of my home like a spoiled brat. I greatly regret that I was silly enough to stop to help you and then to invite you here so you could insult me with your cry-baby behaviour.'

Julia stopped dead in her tracks and turned around, displaying highly aggressive body language.

'You have not the slightest idea in the world about what I am suffering from.'

'Neither do you. Sit down again and don't even think about throwing a vase at me ever again. It's time for you to face up to some real facts for the first time in your life. Your basic problem is a massive overdose of self-pity taken daily in ever-increasing doses for years. Please grow up instead of acting like an idiot twenty-four hours a day, seven days a week.'

Julia looked thunderstruck for a few seconds and looked at the vase again but then totally changed her attitude, sliding down to the floor sobbing as if her heart would break. It took Jessie a while to work out if this was just another act. She decided it was not and walked over to help her up, guiding her to a chair, giving some calm advice as she did.

'Sit quietly for a few minutes. When you feel calm enough, we will work out a plan together.'

The silence lasted a long time. Finally, Julia croaked out some words. 'I suppose that I had better prepare myself to take the first step away from my thoughts about death. Can you tell me, what is the best way for me to do that while rejecting the constant urge to step backwards into darkness?'

'Your very first step is to stop blaming everyone in the world for the disaster your life has become. Say these words to yourself right now, and over and over again, "I have reached the point of wanting to die all by myself. No one has pushed me here. It is all my own fault." You must become like an alcoholic who recovers by constantly telling everyone that she drinks too much and can't help herself.'

'But people did awful things to me year after year.'

'The world has always had those sorts of people, and plenty of them have hit me year after year. I only survived by ignoring them. You generated a terrible hatred of them while at the same time poisoning yourself with self-pity. Now, unpoison yourself. Right now.'

'I can't. They must not get away with what they did. They must be punished.'

'Okay then. Go away and die. There is nothing I can do for you. The blunt fact is that you are grossly selfish. You have spent your whole life thinking about yourself and blaming all the stupid things you have done on everyone else, including your daughter. There's the door. Out.'

There was total silence. Then more quiet sobbing. Then loud sobbing. Then hysteria. Then silence again. No words were spoken. Jessie let silence reign. She had seen too many people lose the plot during her eighty-nine years to let this one worry her.

But Julia made no effort to leave. She seemed consumed by shock. Jessie decided it was time to move things along. 'I am an old lady who always needs a coffee. You need one too. The kettle is on the bench inside, the cups are on the shelf, the coffee is in the cupboard. Go to it.'

Julia was stunned by the request. She thought about it long and hard. Then she slowly rose and walked towards the kettle.

'There are some little pecan pies in the cupboard,' Jessie said. 'Let's eat a few of them. We have earned them.'

Silence once again reigned until Julia returned with all the goodies. Jessie decided to lighten the conversation for a while, so she chatted about the general state of the world, the incompetence and corruption of politicians, and the fact that modern movie stars were not in the same league as Clark Gable and Vivien Leigh or Humphrey Bogart and Katharine Hepburn. Julia had not heard of any of them. Encouragingly, however, she ventured some views about it all.

Jessie reckoned that it was now time to get back to business once more. 'After having experienced intimate relationships with three men, what happened at the end of those troubles that caused you acknowledge you were a lesbian?'

'All my life I have preferred girls to boys,' said Jessie, 'but as I was in trouble with everything else in my life, I did not want to add a major issue to my fragile acceptance by society. This made me think that I should give men a try, so that I looked respectable. Each affair lasted about one month. The first man acted like a rapist. The second guy was kinky. The third could talk only about sex, nothing else. So I walked away from them all, but I think the second guy, the kinky one, is the father of my daughter.'

'From what you said earlier, I am presuming that you never found a woman with whom you could form a strong bond.'

'I was frightened of having a strong relationship with anyone, even my daughter, but I did make an attempt to have a relationship with one woman. But it was just as disastrous as the ones I had with men, maybe more.'

'Why are you and your daughter estranged?'

'She decided that she wanted nothing to do with me or my lifestyle.'

'What caused her to form that opinion?'

'We could find nothing in common, and she was appalled about everything I did, especially my inability to form lasting relationships, even one with her.'

'Where is she now?'

'She is living in a Buddhist community in a very spartan lifestyle. She wears only Buddhist clothing, a brown robe held together by rope and thongs for footwear.'

'Do you ever talk?'

'No.'

'How large are your debts?'

'Not massive, but beyond my capacity to pay.'

'Well, the issue is what we should do about it all?'

'You said we. Was that a slip of the tongue?'

'No.'

'Why we?'

'Because I am a sucker for punishment.'

'Do you realise that you may be about to become the first friend I have had for years?'

'We are not yet friends, but we are going to try to be in the long term. Are you willing to give it a try?'

'I will try.'

'Right, have you got a job at this moment?'

'No.'

'What skills do you have?'

'I did train to be a clerk in a law office. I got work from time to time but always managed to get made redundant.'

'I don't think I can get you any work in a law office, but I can get you a permanent, but very menial, job as a cleaner. It will be hard work and the pay is not great, but we can use it to establish your reputation as a friendly, reliable worker.'

'Wow, are you serious? I think that I will really struggle with doing that sort of work.'

'You really are not in a position to argue, as you don't have many options other than to continue with a few more wrist-slashing exercises. Do you want me to try to get you this job or not?'

Julia stared at the floor. Quietly, she replied in the positive, but she was clearly bewildered as to what was happening to her.

'I will do my best to secure this job for you,' Jessie said. 'If I can, you should be able to pay your rent and buy some food. This being so, are you willing to try to survive for at least three months where you are living now?'

'I think that I should be able to.'

'You will be very welcome to come here to my home for dinner once a week if you wish. We can chat about plans of what might happen after you have three months of settling down.'

'Thank you.'

'I will try to turn on a glass of wine as well.'

'Thank you again. Why are you doing this for me?'

'I have a rare skill. I have from time to time helped a few lame dogs to walk again. I am not suggesting that you are a dog, but I would like to try to get you moving too, as I reckon you can walk a long way if you try.'

Chapter Ten

Jamie was at the airport, en route to Switzerland. He was alone. Last night, he had eaten dinner with Annie at the Country Club on their moonlit veranda restaurant. It was a beautiful occasion, romantic in a unique way that forgot the generational gap. They had held hands, shed tears and drank a very expensive bottle of red wine from the Barossa Valley in Australia.

Jamie had permanently departed from The Haven yesterday, after having personally handed the manager a carefully prepared report. It set out in powerful detail how The Haven was an offence against humanity. He verbally described what was in the report and made it quite clear to the manager that he had no doubt whatsoever that the manager's parents had never married.

The manager panicked in the way that little bullies usually do.

'Can I have an assurance,' the manager said, 'that you will not give this document to the news media?'

'I would not degrade any newspaper by asking them to print a word about you and the company you serve. But I have given a copy of my comments to an influential politician who is appalled to hear what you do. He has decided to conduct a crusade against poorly run aged-care facilities. You will receive a call from him requesting that he make a thorough inspection of The Haven and that you arrange a meeting with the residents. He has promised me that he will be relentless, so my best advice to you is to get smart and start treating residents like human beings. Cease taking money from them for pseudo extras that they don't need. Goodbye and good riddance.'

Jamie took with him only a small travel bag. Annie would collect all his possessions at a later date and decide what to do with them. She would give some to people in need, but she would keep and treasure the old family bible that Jamie had brought with him when he had migrated from Scotland all those years ago. He and Mary had held it when they exchanged their marriage vows. Only one treasure from his past life, other than his memories, travelled with Jamie. It was a lovely portrait photograph of Mary.

Graeme had helped him make prior arrangements to have his ashes scattered from a light plane over the Swiss Alps. Mary's photo would be part of those ashes. Annie would subsequently organise a memorial service for him, and Graeme would give the eulogy a couple of days before he would also die.

Jamie stayed with Annie overnight. They slept in the same bed and did nothing more physical than hold hands all night. It was a hugely comforting experience. In the morning, Jamie travelled alone to the airport in a limo.

Annie had just given him a gentle hug and a kiss, and that was it. They had experienced all the loving goodbyes that they could express on the previous evening at the Country Club. Now, Jamie watched people who were hurrying everywhere to departure gates to catch planes that would within hours scatter them to the uttermost paths of the world. He was headed for the uttermost parts of eternity.

Soon, he was seated in his business class seat, and there was no passenger in the seat beside him. Away the plane soared towards Switzerland. He did not look out of the window to take a last look at the land that he had adopted. The plane staff gave him a nice lunch, which he enjoyed. Black Angus beef from Scotland. He finished with a long black coffee as a myriad of both painful and pleasant recollections from his century alive passed through his mind.

He asked the plane staff if he could enjoy a glass of his favourite liqueur, which happened to be a Drambuie. It was an elegant drink from the Isle of Skye, which was first made by Flora McDonald in honour of Bonnie Prince Charlie when she helped him to escape from the British after losing a bloody battle at Culloden Moor.

As he sipped it slowly, he remembered even more special things about his life, especially those years with Mary. So it was that he slowly drifted to sleep remembering vividly the first time they had made love. It had been an incredible experience that forged their identity as an indivisible one. They still were one.

A few hours later, a hostess looked at him with some concern. She could see no evidence of life. Felt his pulse. There was none. She spoke to him. No answer. Shook him gently. No response. Swiftly, she alerted the captain that they had a dead man on board.

The captain came back with her to Jamie's seat to check for himself. He returned to the cockpit and immediately alerted Zurich Airport. The hostess gently covered Jamie's body with a blanket and alerted the neighbouring passengers about the sad situation.

The truth was that Jamie was searching for Mary and had found her.

Indeed, the hostess noted that he was holding tightly to a photograph of a strikingly beautiful woman. She decided to leave it in his hands.

Chapter Eleven

The bishops' residence was a place that Graeme had always avoided, not solely because it was the habitat of this particular bishop or any other bishop, it was that he had grave doubts that the church needed bishops at all.

He was quite allergic to the whole concept of the way in which churches rated the depth of anyone's Christianity by the titles they gave to those who held any office, clerical or lay. They made it clear that the grander the title you had, the closer you were to God, at least in theory but rarely in practice.

The Most Reverend Matthew Mark loved the splendour of ritual and ceremony and the entitlement of it all, as well as the fine house that went with it. In his case, it was called Bishopsbourne and had been the centre of spiritual power in the diocese for more than a century.

As Graeme approached it, he remembered his ugly battles with the previous bishop, which had been the root cause of him eventually ceasing to be an active parish priest and instead seeking a new Christian vocation as an author.

The Most Reverend Phillip Andrew had been a pompous man, a second-rate leader and a primitively religious politician. He declared himself to be a church man, not an evangelist. He was convinced that society needed a powerful institution like a church if it was to be a stable place in which people could live and move and have their being. Authority was the cornerstone that sustained stability and respect, so long as the Reverend had the authority and received unquestioned respect.

'Leaders' of his ilk had plagued the church and the faith for years. It is a miracle that it survived. This meant that Graeme's style of ministry was totally at odds with that of Phillip Andrew's concept of obedience.

Every progressive innovation that Graeme brought to the life of his parish was the subject of quick criticism from the bishop. He went out of his way to invite dissidents in every parish in the diocese, not just Graeme's, to report to him on the sins of his clergy. This enabled him to let everyone know regularly that he was indisputably in charge, showing that he knew exactly what everyone was doing.

On average, Graeme had been called to Bishopsbourne twice a year to explain himself. He had eventually rebelled and had several blazing rows with Phillip Andrew, which ceased only when the bishop suddenly dropped dead one day. Thankfully, Graeme was nowhere near him when it happened. Many felt that the Lord had struck down the bishop, but Graeme assured them that it really goes without saying that the Lord doesn't do this, even to the worst sinners. Never has and never will. But it was a nice thought.

Graeme often wondered if the bishop found it necessary to be negative and nasty. This made Graeme remember the day during his plentiful travels when he sat in meditation in an old church in England and read a memorial plaque on the wall that had been put there in 1681. It read, 'His religion did not make him unsociable, nor his mirth irreligious.'

Beautiful.

His successor, Matthew Mark, on whom Graeme was calling today, was a vast improvement, but he still fell short of Graeme's view of what a progressive Christian leader should be like. At the very least, he was a decent human being. They got on well with one another and enjoyed a civil relationship. Graeme came with hope that this would continue today.

It was, not surprisingly, a butler who answered the door in response to Graeme ringing the bell. He may well have come right out of *Downton Abbey*.

'Good morning, sir. His Grace is ready and waiting to greet you. Please come this way.'

The butler and his words reminded Graeme that 'His Grace' Bishop Matthew Mark was an eminent leader of the Anglo-Catholic tradition, which was known in earlier times as the High Church. He was very strong on liturgy, tradition and ceremony, and he did it well. But he was not a showman, and he did seem to place a greater value on humanity than he did the church, although not by much. He was a highly educated priest, holding three doctorates with honours from three different universities. They were gained for theology, psychology and history, and he retained a scholarly presence that identified him as a highly intelligent man even though a little aloof. Significantly, he was also the youngest bishop in the history of the diocese. And he looked the part. He never appeared in public without his purple shirt and clerical collar together with a cross around his neck.

Unlike the experience of most mainline churches, attendance at worship in the parishes of his diocese had not declined, mainly due to his personal popularity. But membership had not grown either, and those loyal members were all now ageing rapidly.

The young were significant by their sparse numbers. The absence of youth was not caused by boring sermons from the bishop. Actually, the opposite was the case. His preaching was powerful, intelligent and interesting, but it was locked in a world of two thousand years ago, which had little relevance to people struggling with the massive challenges of the twenty-first century. There was no modern theology in his repertoire.

Bishop Matthew and Graeme exchanged cordial greetings. Matthew insisted that Graeme drop the words 'Your Grace'.

Graeme was struck once more with the dramatic presence of the bishop, a personal asset which was a natural gift. He was of African descent, with his skin ultra-dark and his curly hair even darker. He always wore high-quality shirts and clerical collars, purple being the traditional colour for bishops. With it were pure-white trousers that dramatically highlighted the other colours. Then there were black socks and shoes, always highly polished.

Matthew's parents were Ndebele people who spoke the Bantu language and named their son Mandla—strength, power. They had lived in Matabeleland, which is the southern province of Zimbabwe. His mother was a direct descendent of the last Ndebele kings, Lobengula and Mzilikazi, who lost brutal battles to the British Army who, in the 1890s, conquered their ancient lands for no justifiable reasons other than pure greed. Mandla was only a one year old when his parents fled from their home at the time that Robert Mugabe took over and terrorised the Ndebeles, people he saw as a threat to his power. But Mandla found a place in his new homeland as an outstanding student. His parents anglicised their names, so from Mandla he became Matthew Mark.

Matthew had what could be described as a divided soul. He campaigned aggressively against oppression, racism, sexism, injustice, inequality and poverty, and would continue until his dying days. But he was also a conservative defender of the dogmas and creeds of his church, which he believed were untouchable.

It was Matthew who kicked off the conversation.

'I was surprised when you requested an urgent meeting. As we are both aware, we have met on only a few occasions since I arrived to take up my duties as bishop. You had sought leave of absence from your ministry not long before I arrived here, and this was granted by my predecessor. However, I note with pleasure that, from time to time, you willingly stand in for priests on occasions when they need a few weeks' break. You also have many requests from people who know you to give them spiritual counsel on a wide range of matters. No doubt your incredible fame as an author has helped make you a sought-after friend. So, what is the urgent factor that brings about our meeting today?'

'I have come to tell you that I have only a few weeks left to live. I have terminal cancer.'

Matthew was stunned and genuinely concerned.

'I had noted from your public appearances that you were losing weight and that you were not looking your best, but I had no idea that you were stricken with cancer. I am very sad to hear this and reach out in compassion to you and your family. Are Penelope and Luke and Fiona coping as well as they could hope to from this shock?'

'They are magnificent.'

'I don't know them well, but in my few meetings with them, I found them to be delightful people.'

'I am grateful for your kindness towards me and my family, but I have something else to mention to you, if I may at this point.'

'Please, go ahead.'

'My life will end precisely three weeks from today. I have chosen the path of voluntary assisted dying, and all the legal requirements will be completed well before then.'

'I am lost for words, Graeme, as I hold the firm belief that VAD is a violation of the very basis of our faith, which affirms that there is a creator God who determines the start and end of life. But go ahead and share with me your reasons for doing this.'

'May I discuss the practicality of it first? Then we can talk about my personal theology, which is the core of the framework of my decision.'

'By all means.'

'A panel of eminent cancer specialists have studied my stricken body, and they are unanimous that my life cannot be saved. I have a lethal primary cancer and many secondary ones that have hit vital organs. The situation is quite hopeless.'

'I do not know if I could handle such news personally in any way well.'

'Given that my death at this moment is unavoidable, there is absolutely no point in trying to eke out a few extra weeks of time during which I slowly die under palliative care, not when this is where I do not want to be. It would place huge stress on my family and friends for no valid reason. Also, it simply wastes money that I want my family to have, as all three of them set out to do compassionate work for humanity. We have planned together the innovative projects they will pioneer. So I have simply chosen not to play out time to an inevitable end.'

'Graeme, your action is against our basic belief in a creator God. As I emphasised a moment ago, He starts and ends our creation.'

'I no longer believe in a creator God. I believe only in a God who powers my life spiritually. But if there is a creator God, then he created the cancer that is in me. I am just helping him to finish his own work quickly.'

'God moves in his own way, by means that we cannot often understand. You must not play games with God.'

'Matthew, you will recall that a couple of months ago a young woman and her children were burned to death by a vicious husband and father. You are telling me that this appalling act was God's will?'

'Yes. He was using her to teach us all how dreadful the social scourge of domestic violence is. Her tragic death served a noble purpose.'

'Was it her choice to sacrifice her life in this way? Why did He choose her and not you? If, as you insist, her death was the will of God, then I want nothing more to do with God, as He will be revealed to us as a cold-blooded murderer.'

'Graeme, I am hugely shocked that you, as a priest of God, could bring yourself to say the words you have chosen.'

'Matthew, with considerable respect for you as my bishop, and acknowledging that your scholarship in theology is far greater than mine, let me say with total conviction that God does not decide who lives or dies or who becomes ill and who recovers. Nor does he decide who will be born with a mental or physical difficulty. His sole role is to give us the spiritual power to handle whatever life throws at us. I am utterly convinced that I can handle my cancer and my death because of His power.'

'By saying this, you are destroying the very basis of traditional faith.'

'No, I am not. Quite definitely not. May I ask you this? From what you are saying about the power of God over life and death, you are declaring that God decided that six million Jews and one million Gypsies would die in German gas chambers because Hitler declared they were lesser beings. Do you worship such a God?'

'You are taking this to extremes. That was the work of a madman.'

'But your theology tells you that God created this madman.'

'As you know, Graeme, the will of God has always been a mystery to us.'

'The burning of the woman and her children was not a mystery. It was the work of a madman too, but you said God had a reason for her death. So you are saying that, in the case of the Jews and Gypsies, God had a lapse of memory?'

'Graeme, can we agree to disagree on this?'

'Most certainly, yes, so long as you and I can agree that if God has decided that I am to die from cancer, he won't have any objection to me bringing forward my death by a few weeks, allowing me to die with dignity while causing my family the least possible pain.'

'I accept your right as a Christian to create and sustain your own personal relationship with God.'

'Thank you. Can I make a personal request?'

'Yes, indeed.'

'May I invite you to conduct my funeral service?'

'Do you want to have it in a church?'

'No.'

'Where?'

'In the national park where my ashes will be sprinkled around a tree that my family will plant, not in the exact spot where the tree will be planted, but in the vicinity, as I do not want the tree to become any type of shrine.'

'Agreed. And thank you for the honour of doing so. May I also say that this will be the first time I have had such an experience of ministry.'

'Can I stretch the bonds of our friendship by making a further request?'

'Of course.'

'Can you conduct my funeral service without mentioning eternal life?'

'Why do you request this?'

'Because I do not believe in eternal life.'

'Why not?'

'Because it is a lie.'

'Why is it a lie? Christians have believed in it for two thousand years.'

'Because there is no physical place called Heaven. If there was, then space scientists would have found it by now, as well as assuring us that we will burn to a cinder getting there in a form where we can enjoy an idyllic life. This means that we made the right decision years ago when we embraced cremation instead of rotting for years underground. I am certain that Heaven is the state of mind we live in when we become committed followers of Jesus right here in this world right now, not out in the universe. Eternal life is an even greater lie than claiming the existence of a physical place called Heaven. Scientists tell us that the universe began with the Big Bang about fourteen billion years ago and will probably go on for untold billions of years before it destroys itself. What will you do to entertain yourself for billions of years? Who provides the food and does the washing? Do we do any work in that time? How will we handle billions of years of boredom? It is quite simply nonsense.'

'Graeme, it is our spirit that survives, not our bodies.'

'I agree that our spirit survives our body, but it only survives while our loved ones remember us. We should not promise people that they will one day meet their loved ones and live together happily ever after for billions of years.'

'You can be assured that I will say nothing at your funeral that you do not believe. Nor will I say anything that I don't believe. What words do you want me to use?'

'If you feel that it is appropriate, I would like you to say that I believe that there is a Great Spirit that we call God and from whom I have gained spiritual power. This enables me to become a follower of Jesus of Nazareth and to walk with him along the pilgrim way as together we work to create a compassionate world. I go to my death giving thanks for my life and having complete faith in the Great Spirit. May I specifically ask that you do not seek forgiveness for my sins? It is my responsibility to pay the price of my sins personally before I die by seeking forgiveness from those whom I have hurt.'

'Agreed. May I ask you two questions?'

'By all means.'

'Why do you refer to a Great Spirit?'

'Because I believe that for all people there is a power beyond themselves. Christians call this power God and believe that He sits in judgement of us. I do not believe that He is judgemental in any way. He is a source of spiritual power. If we ignore this power, we live half a life. In addition, most people of whatever culture or religion can identify with a Great Spirit.'

'When you die, what expectation do you have at the moment of death?'

'None. When I am dead, I am dead. That's it. The Great Spirit will neither reward nor punish me.'

'I notice that you always use the words Jesus of Nazareth, not Jesus Christ.'

'The word Christ was invented by the Church to suit its promotional purposes. Jesus of Nazareth was a real man. That's whom I follow.'

'Why do you follow Jesus? We have no means of legally proving that he actually lived. We only have the words of his disciples who witnessed his life and crucifixion, and their thoughts were first recorded seventy years after the event.'

'There come times in life when we must move solely by faith, as we cannot find infallible truth. I adopted Jesus as my role model in life. It is a choice I have never regretted. I am determined to die as bravely as he did. As you and I know, he was going to be killed by the Jewish and Roman establishments, but he chose to go to Jerusalem when he did not need to do so. I firmly believe that he committed voluntary euthanasia. He chose to bring his death forward. I am doing exactly the same.'

'Graeme, you and I are poles apart in theological terms, and we will never reach agreement on what we believe. I took vows as a priest to uphold the creeds and dogmas of the Church and will continue to do so, but at the very least you and I will continue to respect one another.'

'I took the same vows as you did, and I do not for a single moment believe that I have betrayed them. I believe that my calling is to search for truth and to help people open their minds to seek the message that the Great Spirit has for our time, which is an era totally different to the days of the Bible.'

'So, with respect for one another, what do we do next? What do you expect of me between now and your death?'

'I will be very honoured if you will attend a small gathering at my home on the night before my death to share a final drink with me. Then, the day after my death, go with my family and friends to the national park to plant a tree, which will represent the creation of a new life.'

'Done. Both events will be yet another experience I have never encountered before, but I am coming to the view that it will be something special that I, and all others who attend, will always remember. But at this moment, will you pay me the honour of joining me in the chapel for a prayer?'

'Thank you. Lead me there.'

It was a beautifully small chapel. They knelt before the alter. A few moments passed before Bishop Matthew clearly assembled in his mind the words that he felt would suit this special occasion.

> 'Great Spirit, I kneel before you in prayer with my friend Graeme, who has but a short time to live. We are brothers together in your service and we have walked the pilgrim way with Jesus of Nazareth as we have tried to create a compassionate world. There are many things about birth, life and death that are a mystery to us, but we go to our deaths whenever they occur with complete faith in you.

> 'We remember at this difficult time Penelope, Luke and Fiona as they bravely and positively share Graeme's final days. He could not have better partners, and we give our thanks for love they so openly

share. We give our thanks also for the extraordinary ministry that Graeme has expressed through his fine work as a priest of your church, his very successful books about the many ways that people express their faith, his generous philanthropy, and for the powerful inner strength he has to face death with no fear.

'May his spirit live on to the benefit of humanity.

'Amen.'

'Thank you, Matthew.'

'And you, my brother.'

Chapter Twelve

'There is nothing more we can do for him, Aisha. We have absolutely thrown the book at his rare variant of Covid-19 and he continues to decline.'

The infectious diseases specialist who met her at the intensive care unit was emphatic.

'How long do you think he has left?' asked Aisha.

'Hours, maybe minutes. You must call his wife and, if she is willing to risk infection, get her here quickly.'

'She is not able to come. She is in isolation as she has tested positive to Covid-19. Hers is mild compared to that of her husband, but we can't bring her here to this hospital. I will telephone her immediately.'

'After you do that, can I suggest that you go into his room and see him through his death?'

'I will.'

Aisha stood beside Scott's bed. Her discussion with Pauline was very much on her mind. She was a difficult person to deal with and seemed unable to decide whether she should be kind and gentle or harsh and hurtful. In a fury, she had blamed both Aisha and the hospital for incompetence in allowing Scott to reach such a critically low point. Aisha had let her rant on. There was no point in arguing. This woman was out of control. Christian grace totally alluded her.

When the tirade finished, Aisha said, 'You know that your accusations are wrong as well as unchristian. Do you really believe that Jesus Christ would react in the coldblooded way that you have? I regret that I have left Scott alone while I wasted time telling you of his plight.' She had hung up before Pauline could respond.

Aisha's plan had been to get them connected by phone, even if Pauline would only be able to talk. But Pauline had not even requested it, and she was now alone in her selfish world.

Aisha went to have her final consultation with Scott. The intensive care nurses, who were working with determination to save his life, made room for her without ceasing their battle. She sadly noted that the sight of this dying man was filled with a dreadful finality. He was far removed from the dynamo she was used to meeting. He was locked in a dreadful struggle to breathe, and he was about to lose the battle.

His eyes opened and he stared blankly at her. Suddenly, those eyes beamed as though he was in the prime state of his life.

'Need Pauline here,' said Scott. The words came loud and clear without hesitation.

'I greatly regret that I can't arrange that, Scott. She too has Covid-19 and is in compulsory isolation at home, but her affliction is much milder than yours and she has full-time nursing care.'

The light went out of his eyes. 'Give her message.' His words came amid a huge struggle to stay coherent.

'Of course,' said Aisha. 'Gladly.'

This time the words came in gasps. 'God wants her to take up destiny He planned for me. It is his will.'

'I will ensure that she receives and understands your message.'

Now, he really struggled. 'Will I die today?'

'There is a very real danger that you will.'

'Don't want to die.'

'Very few people do, Scott. There is only one that I know. A man called Graeme Brown whom you met yesterday. He did not deliberately choose to die, but he not only accepts that he will die, he has fixed a specific date when it will happen.'

'He is strange.'

'Why do you think that about him?'

'Has different God to me.'

'He has the same God. You just have a different relationship with Him. He is also the same God as I call Allah. My relationship is different too.'

'My God forgot me. Does not need me. Wants my mission to be carried out by someone else, and He has chosen Pauline. I am so pleased about that.'

'I don't know why He would choose to do that. But no matter what reasons He has, you must die with total trust in Him.'

'Am in fear.'

'Don't be.'

'Want to pray.'

'I will join you.'

'God hold me close.'

'Amen,' she said loudly. She held his hand as he stepped across the brink of eternity.

His fading thoughts were not of Pauline. He could hear the splendid music of that beautiful song, 'This Nearly was Mine'. He remembered the painful words, 'Now, now I'm alone, still dreaming of paradise'.

He was unaware that there was, living nearby, a wise old lady called Jessie who also regarded this as her favourite song. He would never have the privilege of meeting her and discovering that she was never alone. This was not possible with six children and 15 grandchildren.

Aisha sat down beside his bed as silently wished him a safe passage. She then thanked the nurses for their sterling work and left the room with a great sense of sadness for a life that had so much potential but was destroyed by a misguided practice of extremist faith.

She went to a computer, completed a death certificate, and signed it. Then she called Pauline once more. She again reacted badly to the news. Even more awfully than their first call, if this was possible.

Aisha hung up for a second time and wondered what she could do to help make a contribution to Pauline's new world. Pauline seemed to be lost somewhere between her life with Scott and her new life without him, and she was blaming everyone else for her dilemma. Or was she pretending that she was grieving and had gone overboard with her expression of it?

Chapter Thirteen

Jessie and Julia looked at their two guests and liked the look of them. Graeme and Penelope had a similar reaction. Just as she had with Graeme and Scott, Aisha marvelled that they had come together. She made introductions in a manner that fostered goodwill all round.

They were in Jessie's little home and were relaxed. Aisha had taken great pains to brief each one of them separately on their respective backgrounds, in the same manner as she had with Graeme and Scott, so they could get down to solid discussions without idle chatter of getting to know one another.

Aisha took the lead. 'Graeme,' she said, 'you have taken legal steps to end your own life because of your terminal cancer. Julia recently tried to take her own life due to severe personal problems that were beyond her capacity to manage.'

Right on cue, and as anticipated by Aisha, Julia intervened.

'Can I clarify this so Graeme and Penelope are aware of the real situation? I clearly and definitely wanted to end my life, but at the final moment I did not have the courage to do so. I staged a non-lethal wrist-slashing so that a passerby, who just happened to be Jessie and whom I had never met before, could be tricked into saving me. On reflection, I was very fortunate that Jessie was that passerby, because she chose to remain in my life and has become my friend.'

Making this statement was a huge step forward for Julia. At long last, she was facing up to the realities of her life.

Graeme had a question. 'If you were so determined to take your own life,' he asked, 'why did you bail out of it at the last moment?'

'I am clear in my own mind that, at this particular point in my life, I really did want to die. My existence had been a mistake and was by every possible standard quite pointless. I went to the park with the absolute intent of ending my life. When I got there, I could not bring myself to do it. I failed in the same way as I have failed at everything else that I have tried to do in my life. I am a non-achiever, just like a rudderless boat.'

This led Julia to follow up with a question of her own. 'You are obviously not afraid of dying, Graeme, because you have arranged a clear and definite date and time for your own death using the legal pathway of voluntary assisted dying. Having tried to die and failed miserably in carrying it out, I have grave doubts that I could bring myself to do what you are about to. From where do you get your courage? Is it based solely on your Christian faith?'

'You have raised a couple of important questions, and I will endeavour to link my answers to both. But feel free to interrupt me if you would like to raise other relevant matters. And this invitation includes you as well, Penelope and Aisha.

Let me start with fear of dying. Firstly, I have never been afraid of dying at any time in my life, but this has nothing to do with bravery. What is the point of being afraid of something that is inevitable in the lives of each and every one of us? None of us can avoid it, no matter what we do or how hard we try. Death is a fundamental part of every life. Logically, as such, we should enjoy it, not fear it. The last day of our lives should be the happiest because there will not be a repeat performance.'

'But', asked Julia, 'why bring it on quicker than you have to?'

'In my case, we are talking about a few weeks. Why place stress on my family when there is no need to do so? After living for about six decades, why worry about a couple of weeks or a month or so? When you decided to try to end your life in a park, did you think about waiting a couple more weeks? Why did you need to bring it on right then?'

'Point taken. You have got me on that one. Thought it'll take me a while to absorb it.'

'As I have said, while I am not afraid of dying, I have been given no option. I am stricken with terminal cancer and, therefore, I have to face the inevitable. So why fear anything that you can do nothing about? What a waste of effort.'

Jessie had a comment from her carefully developed theology of common sense. 'When I got pregnant for the first time out of six, I was frightened. I have got a small body and narrow hips. I could not work out how my baby could have even a remote chance of getting out. I was convinced that I was going to die. When D-Day came and the midwife turned up to my home, I was in mortal fear, especially as I knew I could do nothing about the way that I was born. But I made it, even though I ended up as sore as all hell. Can I say also that the conditions of giving birth did not improve for me the next five times? Except for the fact that I knew for certain that each one would eventually get out. I actually used a bit of common sense and spent time trying to work out how to enjoy it.'

Graeme was warming to Jessie. 'As there is no prospect of me ever getting pregnant, Jessie, I am at a bit of a loss to comment on your fear at that time, except to say that I would prefer pregnancy to cancer. I can only say that your fear had a positive. It was producing a new life. Any fear that I generate about death by cancer will create nothing. I don't believe in life after death, so D-Day for me is a dead end.'

'Well,' responded Jessie, 'if you are ever feeling a bit bored and want to get a few detailed lessons on the pain of childbirth, drop around here for a drink and a pecan pie and a chat.'

'Because I belong to a generation that arrived one cycle later than yours, Jessie, I did have the privilege of sitting beside Penelope in hospital and holding her hand when she gave birth to our twins. But I can't affirm that I really understood the depth of her pain. But I did witness the pride on her face when she held our children in her arms for the first time. I am going to do my best to ensure that she has a similar look of pride on her countenance as she holds my hand while I die. Let me rephrase that. I have not the slightest doubt that she will have a look of love.'

Penelope affirmed that she would have a look of both love and pride at that moment. 'Graeme has found it to be quite hard going,' she said, 'while attending all the meetings with doctors, lawyers, psychiatrists and judges in arranging for the final approval of his death by VAD. He had to face the fact that there was finality in every step. And at the last moment, there will be a final step, which he will have the power at that moment to decline.'

Graeme changed the direction of the conversation. 'What Penelope has said is very true. However, let me ask you this, Julia. Why did you finally decide that you wanted to live? When you took the knife out of your purse to slash your wrists, what happened in that last second that made you decide to miss arteries and just seriously hurt yourself, rather than end your life?'

'My belief in atheism as an alternative to belief in God actually faltered. For a short moment, I wondered if the God I had disowned and rejected might punish me horribly, not only for my hopeless life but also for the sin of suicide. I know now that this was a stupid fear, but I still wondered whether or not the story of being thrown into Hell's fires might be true. I think that this frightened me even more than death.'

'I am still having difficulty understanding your reason for avoiding death, Julia. As an atheist, you will have utterly rejected the possibility of there being any places called Heaven or Hell. I find it hard to believe that you could ever again consider those mythical places to be a possibility, as there are many Christians like me who have never believed that either of them exists.'

'You are a priest of the Anglican Church, and you don't believe in Heaven or Hell?'

'No. Emphatically no. Christianity is not about rewards and punishment. It's about supercharging your life by having a partnership with a spiritual power that is beyond yourself.'

'I think I may need some Christian education from you. Clearly, I am way out of date.'

'No, you don't. You need to work out why you are here in this world and what you want to do about the enormous opportunity this has given you. Mark Twain once said that the two most important days in anyone's life are the day you are born and the day you ask yourself why you were born. So may I ask, without in any way trying to humiliate or denigrate you, why do think you are here in this world?'

'It is a fair question you are asking, but I really don't know the answer. Firstly, I think that I am an accident. I don't think my mother and father intended to produce me or wanted to have me around the place. They were delighted to be rid of me. So I started from a bad place.'

'Millions of people have started from a bad place,' interrupted Jessie. 'Abraham Lincoln had a dreadful start in life. He lived in absolute dirt poverty.'

'Well, as you helped me to understand in our chats, Jessie,' said Julia, 'I was actually pleased that I was poor little me, and now I am disgusted with myself for staying that way for too long.'

Penelope chimed in. 'Now that you have acknowledged that the poor-little-me excuse got you nowhere, what is your reason for living right now?'

'It's turning out to be a tough road to justify my existence. I am trying to prove that I can get and hold a job, provide for my own needs, and then find someone to share my life with. After that, I may be able to find opportunities to be a good citizen.'

'That's a good start,' said Graeme. 'What progress have you made?'

'Can I give you the low down on that?' interrupted Jessie. 'I have been Julia's business partner in this. I told her that she had to start somewhere, and so I helped her get a miserable job as a cleaner. It's awful work, underpaid and boring. She hates it and threatens to resign every second day. But, to her credit, she sticks at it. The money helps pay the rent as well as buy basic foods and a few new clothes.'

It was time for Aisha to get in a word. 'Why are you sticking at this dreadful job, Julia?'

'Jessie has convinced me that I must prove to myself and to future employers that I am a person who can be relied on to stick with a tough job. Jessie made it very clear to me that my previous employment record showed that I was obviously unreliable. I can understand this.'

'Are you willing to improve your skills?' asked Aisha. 'I understand that, at one point in your life, you were qualified to work as a clerk in a law office. Are you able and willing to do more law study so as to requalify and get your old clerk job back?'

'Once I can save enough money to pay the fees, then the answer is yes. I need to requalify as a law clerk, even though this is still a long way from ever being a lawyer.'

'Did you enjoy your work as a law clerk, or was it just a job?' asked Graeme.

'I did like it, but I could not relate to the people I worked with. But I now see that it may have been mostly my fault.'

Graeme came to the point in the conversation where he could act on Aisha's suggestion, one she had thought of after receiving a message from Jessie suggesting that a benefactor may be needed once Julia had proved her worth. 'I want to offer to pay the fees for your retraining as a law clerk,' said Graeme. 'It does not amount to a large sum of money, and I can afford it.'

Julia was stunned. She was quite breathless as she responded. 'I am very grateful for your generosity. May I ask why you are doing this?'

'I am dying. I regard it as a privilege that, at the same time, I can give you the opportunity to have a new life.'

Tears swelled in Julia's eyes. She was bewildered.

Jessie came to the rescue. 'You really must try my pecan pies,' she said. 'I pinched the original recipe from that old American president Jimmy Carter, a person who was a genuine Christian. It has taken me a lifetime to develop it into the perfect recipe and to learn to cook them to perfection. When I die, I want you to promise me that you will put a couple of them in my coffin. You will always find some in the pantry.'

Chapter Fourteen

Aisha was acutely aware that she was not welcome in the Palmer household, and that the same applied to the presence of Graeme Brown. The feeling in the room was electric and darkly negative.

It had taken a persistent effort on her part to arrange a meeting between Graeme, Pauline and herself. Pauline had refused twice, and her refusals had been conveyed in a most unpleasant manner. This was baffling to Aisha, as Pauline had received specific messages from Scott asking her to meet with Graeme. Despite these roadblocks, Aisha had persisted, and Pauline had finally agreed to a 'quick' morning tea at her home.

During this frustrating process, Graeme and Aisha gained the clear impression that Pauline was going out of her way to make sure no one noticed that she was not grieving as much as she ought to under the circumstances. They were coming to believe that her grief was not genuine.

Aisha's campaign had begun when she attended Scott's funeral accompanied by Graeme and Penelope. It could not be held at the huge Pentecostal church at which Scott had been a high-profile and powerful member, because it had been declared a major Covid-19 hotspot after more than two hundred and fifty of its two thousand members had contracted the virus. This was the direct result of their pastor telling them to ignore all the pandemic restrictions. He specifically guaranteed them that their lives were protected by the Lord, as they were His chosen people. In truth, the pastor had received this message from the Lord in a moment of intense prayer.

Twenty-three of those two hundred and fifty had died, three of them having contracted the same variant that had killed Scott. Not only had the church been closed down and heavily fined, their pastor had been jailed for one month for negligence causing death. It was a symbolic gesture by a judge to let the pastor and others know that their faith was not above the law under any circumstances.

Scott's funeral was held at the nearest Pentecostal church to their own, and only one hundred and fifty people were allowed inside so as to adhere to strict physical-distancing rules. Another one hundred were allocated seating on the lawn outside, and this was where Aisha, Penelope and Graeme had been seated. Aisha had done an impressive sales job in convincing Pauline that Graeme's attendance as a world-famous author would draw positive attention to the funeral, as distinct to the hugely negative community reaction that there had been to their Covid-19 tragedy.

Nevertheless, the controversy meant it was necessary to organise a livestream so that thousands of others could watch the funeral from their homes and offices. It turned out to be quite an event. Pauline had spent an impressive amount paying a revered singer, a choir and several religious celebrities to preform virtually from afar. She promoted it actively on every form of social media that existed and then livestreamed it, thus ensuring that Scott did not die unnoticed and that she too would be noticed.

She was hard to ignore—tall in contrast to Scott, who was short in stature—and looking like a blueblood. She gave the eulogy herself, showing just the right amount of grief so that she could set the stage for her own future.

———

The trio had a brief word with Pauline before they left the funeral, but her response was curt, cold and rude, letting them know that they had been granted a special privilege in being allowed to attend, a privilege denied to true believers who really deserved those seats.

Now Aisha and Graeme were at the Palmer home, seated in a beautifully furnished lounge room that had been made possible solely by the endless financial blessings of the Lord.

Pauline made it obvious that she was not happy to have them in her home. 'Scott and I, and our fine church, have been humiliated by this tragedy, and it seems that the whole city is laughing at us, including people like you.'

Graeme responded quietly. 'Some people are mocking you, Pauline, but they are the same ones who mock the entire world about anything that they feel they can ridicule. I do not take them seriously, and I strongly recommend that you ignore them too.'

'I cannot believe that our pastor has been charged, found guilty at a humiliating trail, and then jailed. I know him to be one of the finest spiritual leaders in the world right now. As he emphatically told the court, he did receive a clear message from the Lord after intense prayer affirming that we are God's people and were under his special protection due to our years of devoted worship and service. He could do nothing else but to listen to the Lord and report what He said. There is something very wrong about it all. The court that declared him guilty has become an agent of the Devil. I pray for an answer to it all a dozen times a day. But no clear message comes from God. We are in a spiritual desert. I am quite lost, just as Scott was. Everything has been incredibly meaningless.'

'No, you are not lost, Pauline,' said Graeme. 'Your church members made a basic human error. God did not let you down, nor did He punish you. He has now clearly told you that you have not been acting as responsible Christians. You were arrogant, and in doing so, you insulted everything that God stands for. Christians care for other people first, themselves second, and they always act responsibly. Your church did not follow any of those principles. You created circumstances in which people died. All you need to do to please God right now is to pledge to never do such an irresponsible thing again.'

'Do you really believe that, or are you ridiculing me?'

'I believe it, and so should you. And as you are fully aware, neither Aisha nor I have ever ridiculed you or ever will. We are making honest comments about a tragedy that your church must now repair.'

'Forgive me, I am having trouble absorbing all of this.'

'Take your time. Neither you nor your church have a future until you accept your mistakes and believe and accept that our faith is inevitably linked to the care and responsibility of others. I don't intend to hurt you with this comment, but there is a very real chance that Scott would still be alive today if your church had acted responsibly right from day one of the pandemic. But the important thing now is to work out how you and your church can start again and build a new life out of the ashes of this disaster.'

'You are asking me to give up the basic elements of my faith that have been the cornerstone of my life. Like our pastor, I do believe that I am one of God's chosen people and that He has given us prosperity. The Bible promises it.'

'Jesus also promised it to slaves and prostitutes and tax collectors, and the God you worship has made it clear in recent weeks that you and your church need to reassess whether or not you really are His chosen people.'

'You have no right to place me and others who are chosen people on the same level as those disgraceful people you just compared us to,' screamed Pauline as she totally blew a fuse and threw her cup of hot tea at Graeme's face.

Her throw was very accurate, but Graeme did not flinch. Pauline then turned her attention to Aisha and threw a plate at her. Aisha ducked and it smashed into the wall behind her, pieces flying everywhere. Not that it mattered to Pauline, but the plate was part of a rare, expensive and irreplaceable set.

Keeping his cool, Graeme's calmly replied, 'I am presuming that the Lord called upon you to do that too?'

Aisha rushed to his aid and made a brief examination. 'The tea hit your forehead and your scalp. Your eyes look okay. You must have blinked at the right moment. I have some medication in my doctor's bag in the car. I will get it and do what I can to ease the burning.'

Pauline still had a look of fury, showing no remorse and making no move to help Graeme. Graeme decided that some appropriately direct words were necessary.

'Pauline, you are a disgrace to your God and your faith. Indeed, you are a total sham.'

'I admit that I should not have done that, but you deserved it. Not only have you demeaned my faith and my church, but I have been told that you will shortly commit suicide using the shocking legislation that allows people like you to end your life by the cynical means called voluntary assisted dying. This procedure is the ultimate evil. It is an offence to God.'

'Your intent, Pauline, was to hurt me, firstly with hot tea, then with vicious words. You have failed badly on both counts. Let me say that the burns you have inflicted on my head are quite insignificant in comparison to the constant pain that my several cancers create. And the evil of which you accuse me about voluntary assisted dying is sheer hypocrisy on your part. If I accept your theology that only God decides who dies and when, then God decided that I would die of cancer, and I have accepted His decision. I am simply bringing forward the date when His decision will be achieved. On the other hand, you have not accepted God's decision to end Scott's life, and you are indeed bitter in your rejection of His decision. At this moment of your life, are you in God's team or not?'

Pauline flared once more, but this time she was hot from embarrassment. Graeme's comment had for all intents and purposes speared her through the heart. She was about to launch a defensive tirade when Aisha interrupted, having returned to work on Graeme's burns.

'You, Pauline, are not a Christian,' said Aisha. 'You never have been and never will be. You are a total fraud and a vicious bigot. Can I suggest, with all the goodwill I am having extreme difficulty in mustering, that you totally and honestly re-examine your life and make a supreme effort to learn what Christianity is all about.'

Pauline flared again, looking around for something else she could throw. Aisha walked calmly towards her and slapped her face hard, using the hand that still had some burn cream on it. It splattered everywhere, making a mess of Pauline's expensive dress.

Pauline tried to hit back. Missed. She sank back into her chair and went totally silent.

Graeme spoke while Aisha continued to work on his burns. 'I will leave here shortly as this, Pauline, is clearly your wish. Aisha will leave with me. However, before I do, I want to arrange to have a discussion with you about the message that Scott sent to you a few minutes before he died. He wants you to carry out his Christian mission. You cannot and must not ignore this, as I gave Scott a personal commitment that I would talk to you about it in detail. Could I suggest that I return to meet you here tomorrow at this time? I have given much thought to my promise to Scott, and I have advice on how I believe Scott would want you to act. I am suggesting tomorrow because I have very few days left. Will you meet me to plan how you can honour the man you loved and still do? Our meeting will be on the basis that no bitter words and condemnation will pass between us. We will confine ourselves to discussing constructive plans.'

Silence. Then a one-word response. 'Yes,' said Pauline.

'Aisha will now drive me home. I will come alone tomorrow. May I also say that I am holding drinks for friends at my home on the afternoon before I depart this life by voluntary assisted dying. I will bring you an invitation tomorrow, and I hope you will come. Before I die, I would like to know that we part as friends.'

Graeme did not wait for a response. He and Aisha left. Pauline did not rise from her chair, staring instead at a portrait of Scott. Her turmoil was severe and confused. She was struggling with the strength of her relationship with Scott, alive or dead.

After a while, a moment of clarity arrived. There was a possibility that she could turn Scott's death into the platform for her future, something that was always second fiddle while Scott was around.

Chapter Fifteen

The Donald looked Graeme squarely in the eye.

'Welcome to my worldwide audience, Graeme. Every one of us wants to know why you have decided to commit suicide and to do so in such a public fashion.'

The Donald was Donald Goldwater, host of a talk show called *The Donald At Large*. It was reliably estimated to have the world's largest media audience. It spread its tentacles from New York to more than one hundred nations by television, radio, podcast, social media and so on.

Goldwater got his break into worldwide fame as a broadcaster when he was working on both radio and television at a place called Sandy Hook in Connecticut, USA, at the time that a mass shooting took place. By sheer good fortune to his future career, he just happened to be at the scene of the ghastly crime at the exact moment it happened, becoming its spokesman to the world. He cashed in on this fluke of fame by spending every dollar he had employing a career manager who got him jobs and contracts far beyond Sandy Hook. He never looked back.

Though separated by many thousands of kilometres, The Donald and Graeme were talking to one another in a virtual studio where it was impossible for viewers to work out that they were in reality continents apart.

Graeme was seated in a lounge chair at his home looking very relaxed with a scotch whisky at hand. Penelope had done a competent job with her cosmetics to cover up Graeme's hot-tea blisters, and Luke and Fiona had handled the electronics that connected him to The Donald after a detailed briefing from his production team.

The host deliberately called himself The Donald so as to cash in on Donald Trump's now fading legend. Many viewers who listened without seeing him actually thought he was the original Donald, and Goldwater did nothing to correct this misunderstanding. He had many of the same outrageous attitudes as Trump anyway but was ten times more intelligent— even though he too reflected Trump's propensity for irresponsible crudity.

That cunning nous led The Donald to believe that his program thrived because of his objectionable style of interviewing, and that his future depended on him perpetuating it. There were never any kind questions asked of anyone who appeared on The Donald's show. He was a prime example of the way in which the media now dominated the culture of the world, for good or bad, and how few had the will or the power to change it.

Graeme had refrained from any public comments on his cancer and its finality. Nevertheless, his fame as an author meant that it inevitably leaked. Up until now, he had rejected all interviews with any media outlet. Finally, he decided on one appearance only and had deliberately chosen to speak with The Donald because the great star had called him personally on three occasions and had an audience that easily surpassed all others in followers and global reach. His high profile meant that Graeme had no chance of stopping public debate about his impending death.

'Hello, Donald,' said Graeme. 'Thank you for inviting me to chat with you today. May I respond to your question by indicating that someone has misinformed you? I am not planning a suicide.'

'Come on now, Graeme. Just pause a moment while I tell our viewers and listeners the exact day, time and place when you will commit suicide.'

The Donald did, then added, 'You have undeniably set a suicide date. Why deny it?'

Graeme had told only a few people the exact details of his death, but as several doctors, lawyers and public servants had a role in approving his application for voluntary assisted dying, he guessed that one of them had leaked it.'

'Because it's not suicide?' responded Graeme.

'Don't lie to me, Graeme. You know that's not a smart tactic to use on my program. This clearly is suicide, and I will not allow you to avoid the question.'

'Please define the word suicide for me, Donald. We seem to have different views of what constitutes suicide.'

'Come on again, you know the answer better than I do. But I will humour you. Suicide occurs when a person takes his or her own life. That is it. Game, set and match.'

'Come on now yourself, Donald. Finish the definition. Add the words "in circumstances beyond the law". My life will end in accordance with the law. Voluntary assisted dying is provided for in the laws of my nation. Those laws on VAD have been challenged in the courts, but the judges rejected the challenges, declaring VAD to be lawful. It is not suicide. It just brings forward the date of an inevitable death, the cause of which for me is cancer.'

'Stop playing with words.'

'I am not. You are trying to use the word suicide emotionally, not legally. You should not play around with the legal decisions of parliament and courts. Can we get on with this interview? Your millions of listeners are getting bored with your behaviour. You could be doing perilous harm to your ratings.'

'Nonsense. Your pathetic responses to my valid questions are boosting my ratings by the second. Why are you committing voluntary assisted dying?'

'It is quite simple really. Five highly skilled and experienced medical professionals have affirmed that I am quickly dying from several virulent cancers, and I now have just a short time to go at the most. Three psychologists have certified that I am sane. So I have decided not to subject my family to the trauma of sitting beside me every day as I die while being drugged out of my mind, unaware that they are there. I will hold a pleasant farewell wake with them and close friends, then die the following day. My family will be with me.'

'But if you hang on to life for a while, the cancers may go into remission, or there might be a miracle cure that saves you.'

'There won't be. My body is riddled with cancer. I am doomed to die. I am bringing forward the inevitable and not creating an additional death. How can this be suicide? Will you be more at peace if I stage a car accident on a lonely road and make it look as though I died a tragic death? This is a daily occurrence throughout the world.'

'Why die before you have to?'

'In a life of sixty years, why do a few weeks have any value?'

'Most people sign up for palliative care when they have cancer. Why don't you do the same?'

'Because I don't want to sit in a chair or lie in a bed looking like a zombie or a vegetable.'

'Well, surely that is better than dying?'

'It's far worse. Considerable social research has been done on palliative care, and it shows that an overwhelming number of people in palliative care suffer mental stress because they don't want to be in that state. Sadly, their families and their doctors have forced them to be there.'

'What is wrong with a family wanting to keep a loved one alive?'

'Because it is not their decision.'

'That's a vindictive comment.'

'It is not. It just states the truth. The best course to follow is to combine palliative care with voluntary assisted dying. That way people are kept out of pain while going through the legal processes required to arrange voluntary assisted dying.'

'You are too smart for your own good.'

'No, just practical.'

'Surely your wife and family tried to talk you out of this. They must be outraged.'

'They are not. We made the decision together. I have their one hundred per cent support. We are immensely enjoying the quality time we have shared over these last few precious weeks.'

'Are you living in dread of this horrible event?'

'No.'

'You are putting on a show for me and my listeners so as to get us all to revere you as a brave man.'

'I am not a brave man. I am a dying one.'

'You are telling me that you are not in any way afraid of death?'

'No.'

'Why are you not afraid?'

'It's pointless being afraid.'

'Oh, for God's sake, why is it pointless?'

'Because one day it's going to happen to you personally, Donald, as it will to me and every one of our listeners, wherever they may be. It is unavoidable. So why fear it? Why not enjoy it? I have been given clear notice of its occurrence for me personally, so what is wrong with making it a happy send off? Will we all feel better if I sit and cry my eyes out when I do not believe that my cancer and my death are not unfair?'

'I know why you are so relaxed about it. As you are a Christian, you think you are going to Heaven and so you are happy to get there. I am not a practising Christian and never will be, so what's in it for me?'

'Absolutely nothing. And there is absolutely nothing in it for me either. I do not believe in life after death or in there being physical places such as Heaven and Hell.'

'No wonder they kicked you out of the church. How can you be a Christian and not believe in life after death and in Heaven and Hell?'

'Because to be a Christian all you need to do is become a committed follower of a man called Jesus of Nazareth. Nothing else. There is no life after death, because when die you are dead. You become ashes either immediately or later. You are not going anywhere. Heaven is not a place somewhere out in space. Heaven represents your lifestyle right here and now when you become a follower of Jesus. Hell is the negative mindset you acquire when you choose to ignore him.'

'Your bishop must be cranking up the rack ready to put you on it permanently.'

'I will be rather surprised if he does. And for the record, I have not been kicked out of my church. I am a priest in full standing. I conduct worship when invited and I am authorised by the bishop to give all the sacraments. I do this because I am a devoted follower of Jesus of Nazareth even though I do not believe in the creeds and dogmas that have been adopted by the church. I don't believe that Jesus believed them either. His ministry was to real people, not words of fear put in a book by a church.'

'When the bishop watches this program, he will not only put you on the rack, he will boot you out of his church forever. He won't put up with your heresy and theological nonsense anymore.'

'He already knows all about the matters you and I are discussing today. I have visited him personally to discuss these issues with him in considerable detail.'

'What did he decide to do with you?'

'He accepted my invitation to come to my farewell party.'

'I can fully understand that. He is delighted to see the end of you. He will be the happiest chap at that party, grinning from ear to ear while he enjoys drinking your free booze.'

'I am sure he will enjoy the occasion, as will all of my guests.'

'No wonder churches are now irrelevant when they condone people killing themselves and get drunk while approving it.'

'Let me ask you a question, Donald. Why are you not a Christian?'

'Because every word of it is bullshit. Churches are places where the frightened gather so they can get more frightened. They think that when they get to Heaven, everything will be lovely forever. Well, if it is so lovely, why the goddam hell aren't they busting their gut to get there? Most of them are total frauds.'

'Well, what do you believe in, Donald? What is the basic cornerstone of your life?'

'Honesty. Decency. Looking after my friends. Helping a few decent people get out of the gutter. Terrorising politicians who don't do their job or have their fingers in the till. Those basic things that are important to good people.'

'I agree with all of those things too, Donald. I am a conservative, not a radical. I defend and promote and conserve all that is true, right, noble, lovely and admirable. So why are we not friends?'

'Because you say you are a Christian but then go out of your way not to talk and act like one. Because you play around with big issues like dying when you don't have to. And you won't answer direct questions. You pretend you are an intellectual just so you can avoid the tough questions.'

'So, facing up to death is not a big issue?'

'You are playing games with it.'

'I would not say that pressing a lethal button at a hospital that will instantly kill me can reasonably be described as playing games. However, let me ask you this, Donald. What will happen to you when you die?'

'Have not got a clue. Not interested. But I am going to make sure I don't go anywhere there may be any Christians.'

'If I was you, Donald, I would not be too concerned about this happening. Let me say this. You may find it helpful. When I press the lethal button, it will kill me and my cancer but it won't kill my spirit. What happens to that spirit, which is actually me, is a mystery, but I think it lives on in the hearts and minds and souls of those who love me. I do hope there are people out there who love you as distinct from being entertained by you.'

'Can I, Graeme, ram home this undeniable truth? You are too smart for your own good, so let us finish this interview. Millions of viewers out there think you are a total nutter.'

'Before you do, Donald, can you give me some statistics of reactions from those listeners right now? You must have stirred up a huge volume of calls, texts and emails after your extraordinary tirade.'

'Okay, let me call in my manager. Charlie, get in here. What is the audience reaction to this crazy interview?'

Charlie appeared. He seemed pleased to be able to give The Donald the news that he was about to give him. 'You are not winning this one, Donald. Eighty per cent of our callers reckon that Graeme is a splendid fellow who is doing a brave and noble thing. Most say they hope they will have the same courage when they face their own imminent death.'

'Oh God save us. What is happening in the world out there?'

Graeme had what he hoped would be the last word. 'I have to leave you right now, Donald. My wife Penelope and I have a meeting to go to shortly that relates to the final approval of my application for voluntary assisted dying. I will send you an invitation to my farewell party. You will be genuinely welcome there. I look forward to having a final chat with you and to saying a pleasant farewell. You can fly here and back in your executive jet quite easily.'

'If you should happen to see me arrive at your party, which is highly doubtful, you will know that I have reached such a crazy point in my life that I can't resist being at the strangest celebration ever held anywhere at any time in history. It may be that my listeners out there who say they love you may demand a personal report from me on your final curtain call.'

Graeme continued in his quest to get in the last word. 'With regard to the staging of final curtain calls, can I ask if you are a fan of Ulysses S. Grant, former president of your nation one hundred and fifty years ago?'

'Absolutely, a great hero of our Civil War. He healed the great divisions that had ripped our nation apart.'

'He died of cancer. When his doctors told him that they could do no more to save him, he decided to write his memoirs so he had a goal that would help him not to think of his death. He worked at it relentlessly.

One thousand pages in all. Every one hand-written. The intensity with which he undertook the task took a toll on his heart, and he died much sooner than he should have. It was a clear case of voluntary euthanasia. Sadly, his death occurred before he could publish it. A great man stepped forward. Mark Twain. He got it published and made sure that Grant's family got the royalties. Think about that before you come to my farewell party. Bye for now. Over and out.'

———

Barton Deakin was disgusted. He was sitting at his desk at the Law School of St Andrew's University where he had for two decades been dean. Of medium build and with a magnificent beard, he gazed out across the lawns to the bell tower that guarded the gates of this revered place of learning.

His seventy-year-old mind was an orderly one that expressed logical clarity at all times. He had just been grossly offended and disturbed by the words that The Donald had used in his public altercation with Graeme Brown a few minutes ago. The guy was an arsehole. These were words that he rarely used, especially within these hallowed halls of learning, but this moment called for them.

He had a couple of profound thoughts about The Donald. Firstly, he acknowledged that the man marketed himself superbly. He had an audience of many millions across the world. Most of them worshipped him, but there was a sizeable number who listened for the sole purpose of being shocked, thus able to discuss it all later with indignation and horror over coffee or drinks. He was a fundamental element in their quest to sound intelligently relevant. A much smaller number of his audience were actually intelligent, listening so as to be able to objectively analyse the effect The Donald was having on world opinion, and what they should do about it, if anything.

Secondly, the guy had an interesting interviewing technique. He was deliberately and provocatively rude, with an ability to convey the impression that he was only being rude because his victim deserved it and that he, The Donald, on behalf of humanity, was defending all that was decent. It was a decadent style, but brilliant.

Barton's admiration of him stopped right there. He was appalled that Donald Goldwater had accused Graeme Brown of intending to commit suicide. Voluntary assisted dying is absolutely and fundamentally legal. It never has been suicide, never will be suicide.

In Barton's view, the word suicide was used by VAD opponents as a highly emotive and hurtful word designed to create maximum distress to proponents and users of VAD, because those opponents have no valid argument against it. They use the suicide accusation as a last-resort king hit, invoking the name of God as they do so, even though they know that their lying words were enormously unchristian. Barton was convinced that all opponents of VAD were frightened little people who lived in fear of dying. They didn't want it ever discussed in their presence, and whenever it was, they lashed out blindly and bitterly.

Barton was certain that The Donald was scared of dying and had worked out that most of his listeners were too. So he played to their fear, as this helped to sooth his own fear. The guy was a gutless wimp, and wimps had no place in Barton's life.

He hoped that Goldwater would accept Graeme's invitation to his wake. Barton had been invited and had instantly accepted it as a huge honour. He had enormous regard for Graeme Brown. Barton loved spending time with great minds, and Graeme's mind was overflowing with knowledge, wisdom and faith. Graeme had over the past decade accepted every invitation from Barton to give lectures on ethics to his students and staff, and they had always been one of the highlights of the year. In between lectures, he had always welcomed Graeme as his guest at dinners at the university club when eminent international scholars were visiting the campus.

Even though Graeme had conducted himself well in the interview with The Donald, the wake would be an appropriate opportunity to take the broadcaster down a well-deserved peg or two, and to more than level the score for his friend.

Chapter Sixteen

Fiona and Luke found it hard not to stare. Julia's daughter, Sarah, was Buddhist, and there she was before them, wearing sandals and dressed in a Buddhist's traditional brown robe tied with string. There was not even the slightest hint of make-up or polish on her nails. Her hair was short, straight and plain but well cared for.

Sarah took the initiative in opening the conversation.

'Thank you for taking the time to meet me. I feel very honoured to be with you.'

'We have been looking forward to the occasion too, Sarah,' responded Fiona. 'And now that we are here, we are sure that it will be a delightful and interesting time together. May we join in the happy greetings and add that this is the first time we have met a Buddhist in person?'

The meeting had been secretly organised by Jessie Windsor. It was she who had suggested it to Aisha, as she felt that Sarah would respond to meeting with two young people. Aisha then called Julia to get contact details for Sarah. This information proved to be out of date, but Jessie was nothing if not persistent. She followed up every lead from the initial details she had until she finally located where Sarah was, but she refrained from making direct contact herself.

Jessie discussed her findings with Aisha, who devised a complicated process that she soon put into action. Firstly, Aisha called Graeme, who discussed it with his children. They reluctantly agreed to a meeting, mainly because they wondered how violent the relationship had been between Julia and Sarah and who was most at fault. Aisha then went to see Sarah, unannounced and uninvited, as she was aware that Sarah never responded to any contacts from her mother, as she had firmly closed the doors to her past life. Eventually, the meeting was arranged. Sarah was a reluctant participant, but she warmed to Aisha and felt she could have confidence in her advice. Jessie suggested that the meeting take place in the very park at which Julia had tried to take her own life.

They were sitting on a blanket on the grass near the seat on which the attempted suicide had occurred. Luke and Fiona were aware of how the attempted suicide had played out, though Sarah was not. Aisha had told her that her mother had experienced some serious personal issues, and that Luke and Fiona were good Samaritans who were trying to help solve some of her problems. This was doubly difficult for them because Fiona and Luke had never met Julia. They relied solely on extensive briefings from Graeme and Aisha.

Luke decided that he should begin to lead the conversation towards the crunch matter.

'It may be helpful,' he said, 'if we start our time together by sharing a brief background of our lives? Fiona and I are twins, born twenty-two years ago. We are both at university. Fiona is in the final year of her studies for a double degree in journalism and law. She hopes to become an investigative journalist. I still have a long way to go in completing my studies in science and medicine. I want to become a scientist specialising in research into all aspects of longevity.'

'I chose journalism,' Fiona said, 'not just because I want to be a great writer like our father. I want to be at the forefront of a new era in writing that rises above sensational journalism, replacing it with quality reading that becomes a real learning experience for readers. We get our enthusiasm for learning and communicating from our mother, Penelope, who is the principal of an interfaith college.'

Sarah responded thoughtfully, 'I did not do well at school, mainly because I did not do well at home, but I now realise that I was wrong just to accept my state of life. I gave up study without ever qualifying for entry to a university or any profession. But by a stroke of good fortune, I got a job as a clerk in the office of a businessman who is a Buddhist. He never tried to influence me to accept Buddhism, but his sincerity impressed me so I decided to take up the Buddhist way of life. This led to me being invited to begin work as a helper in a Buddhist home for the terminally ill, where we try to help people die well. I am only nineteen years old, and I have a lot to learn.'

'That', said Fiona, 'has been an interesting life journey. Other than for the example of your mentor, why did you choose to become a Buddhist? Having been born into a Christian home, I never thought of not being a Christian.'

'Thank you for inquiring. Very few people do. They just quietly think that I am odd, and I probably am. It was an easy decision as I was never a Christian at any time of my life. Nor was I ever of any other faith. As my life was always unstable, I was interested when my employer told me that Buddhists believed that nothing was permanent and that everything changes. I learned that the goal of life for a Buddhist was to find enlightenment. We do this by finding the good actions that are set out in the Eightfold Path. I am just starting my journey.'

'I would like learn more about that', responded Luke sincerely.

'I am still on a steep learning curve, but as I understand it, the Eightfold Path is a life-long journey that separates severe self-discipline from total indulgence. It begins with a basic understanding of the nature of things and moves through the challenge of doing things correctly by intention, speech, action, livelihood, effort, mindfulness and concentration. Within any one of those matters there are a very wide range of issues to be mastered, so I am on a long, interesting and challenging journey. The self-discipline fundamental to progress is good for me.'

'Thank you, Sarah, I will follow that up with some more reading. I have an avenue to do this through my mother's work as the leader of the College of Abraham, where there are some Buddhist students. In the meantime, we would be very interested to learn why you chose to work at a home for the terminally ill. We are especially interested because our father, Graeme, is terminally ill and has only a short time to live.'

'I am sorry that your father is so ill. Pain is something that I have always feared. I can't explain why, but it always has been a factor in my life. Therefore, I have a very compassionate attitude to those who are in pain. This again drew me to Buddhism, as it promotes strong feelings of care for those who are dying in pain. We place a lot of emphasis in preparing people for death itself, as we do not believe that there is life after death. We believe that we immediately return to the world in another form, and that it may not be human. I very much relate to this, and so I love my work at the Buddhist hospice. But please, tell me about your father. When Dr Aisha met with me to suggest our meeting, she mentioned him and said that she hoped we would talk about his death, as she believed that it will be a quite special end for a wonderful person.'

'Graeme is a special person,' Fiona responded. 'He is an ordained Anglican priest who, some years ago, asked for and was granted leave of absence from his duties so that he could become a full-time author. He has been highly successful at that.'

'I discovered that your father was a famous author,' Sarah said, 'and a fine human being after Dr Aisha mentioned him. I typed his name into Google and discovered that his career as an author has been recognised positively worldwide. You must be very proud of him.'

'We are, and now we also have a loving relationship as we are walking with him on his final journey. It is a challenging time for us, as he has chosen a specific date for his death via voluntary assisted dying.'

'Dr Aisha mentioned that too. At first, I was shocked, but then I began to think that a decision such as he has made is something like the enlightenment we seek as Buddhists. He seems to be welcoming death because he does not fear it. It takes a very mentally strong person to do this.'

'Thank you for that supportive comment, Sarah,' said Luke. He continued by raising the matter that was the fundamental reason for this meeting in a park. 'Can we speak about your mother for a few minutes, Sarah?'

'Certainly, Luke and Fiona, but I do not know much about her life now. Three years ago, when I was just sixteen, I left her and have had no contact since. I have not tried to be in touch with her in any way, as I have no wish to meet her again. However, I am here because Dr Aisha said you would give me some important information about some serious problems she is now facing.'

Luke took heart from this open response and got down to serious business. 'We have never met your mother, but we have been given reliable information about her by a wonderful old lady called Jessie who has befriended her. Aisha arranged for Jessie to meet us so we could be briefed on the details. A couple of weeks ago, your mother tried to commit suicide one evening right here in this park, at the very place where we are now sitting. Jessie happened to be walking through the park at the time and saved her. Now Jessie is spending lots of time helping your mother while she begins to undertake the huge task of rebuilding her life. She seems to have begun a slow but steady passage forward as she learns how to build personal relationships.'

Sarah bowed her head in silence. Luke and Fiona kept their silence.

'I think that it is fair to say that I am responsible,' said Sarah.

'Why?' asked Luke.

'Julia and I never liked one another, almost from the moment that I was born. I never felt secure with her, and for many years I planned to leave her at the first opportunity I could find that would give me a chance of survival. Other children seemed to have lovely mothers, but I did not. I spent my whole life looking for someone who I could love and trust. I am still looking. My Buddhist friends have cared for me wonderfully and are always opening new doors for me, but I do not have a close relationship with anyone. I assume that my negative attitude towards my mother must have had some part in her trying to kill herself.'

'So why did you leave her three years ago?'

'I had reached a point when it was time. I went to see the Salvation Army, and they took me in. I stayed at a girl's hostel they managed, and I got part-time work in their coffee shop so I could pay for rent and basic foods. I survived well, and it was a wonderful break when I got work with the Buddhist man I mentioned earlier.'

'Have you had any contact with your mother since you left?'

'No.'

'Can I ask,' said Fiona, 'why you finally decided to become a Buddhist, rather than become a member of the Salvation Army? After all, they cared for you for a couple of years.'

'The Salvation Army did care for me, and I am grateful to them for they are good people. But I rejected any thought that there was a God who cared for me because I could find no evidence of either His presence or His value. I found the quest for enlightenment as a Buddhist to be a far more challenging and meaningful experience than I ever found in the Bible studies that the Salvation Army held. Buddhism has taught me to look after myself and has guided me to care for others even more so, especially those who live in pain.'

Luke raised the crucial question. 'Would you like to meet your mother again, face to face?'

Sarah looked up into the sky as if looking for enlightenment about this challenge. 'My most frank and honest answer is that I don't want to, but I also really don't know what I should do. I cannot see any need for her to have a presence in my life, or that she has any need of me in her life. But I cannot avoid the undeniable fact that she is my mother, and that she must have experienced awful crises that caused her to try to end her own life. So this means that I must have some sense of responsibility in my life to do something about it. The problem is that I have a real dilemma as to what to do.'

'We think that we could help you to arrange a meeting,' Fiona said.

'Did my mother ask you to arrange a meeting?'

'To the best of our knowledge, your mother knows nothing about our meeting today. The wonderful person, Jessie, who we mentioned earlier, organised it all through Dr Aisha without telling your mother. She got the idea when Aisha arranged for our dad to meet Julia recently. She has taken a huge risk, as it is highly possible that your mother may be furious if she discovers what has happened.'

'I am willing to give it a try, so long as it is at a gathering place where others are in attendance, so that she will be deterred from making a scene.'

'Wonderful,' said Fiona. 'Leave it to us to work out a way, and we will get back to you to check that you find it acceptable. Jessie will be a real help in organising this. She is a wise one. Quite a nice person. But let's change the subject now and chat about what music we like and what books we read. Luke and I are real fans of Elton John, not just for his music but for his great work as a philanthropist. We also love reading books written by David Attenborough. We want to help him save the planet.'

'I don't have much interest in books or music. It is a defect in my life that you may be able to turn around.'

This topic was a relaxing diversion and continued for quite a while as they enjoyed the coffee and cakes that Fiona had brought along. This friendship had more long-term possibilities than a revival of a relationship between Sarah and Julia. However, time is forever a great healer.

Chapter Seventeen

Pauline looked ghastly. She was both unhappy and confused but not hostile or remote. Her attitude was one of unease. She seemed to have much on her mind.

Graeme was still somewhat blistered by the hot tea of yesterday, but while still discomforted, he remained calm, focused and positive. As Pauline had made no effort to apologise or even appear to be concerned about her behaviour, Graeme decided to get started immediately on the agenda for their meeting that had been agreed upon yesterday. Idle chatter would be pointless, as was the possibility of a friendship.

'When I met with him just before his death,' Graeme said, 'Scott asked me to confirm his message to you, which is that he wants you to carry on his mission that he passionately believed God had given him to do. So as not to waste time in this meeting with matters that may distress you, may I suggest that you commence planning to use the wealth that you and Scott have accumulated via many years of hard work to carry out the work of your own ministry, not Scott's?'

He was anticipating that Pauline would explode in righteous indignation and protest at the very thought of not honouring the noble calling that Scott had followed, but he was not at all surprised when she did not. Silently, he pondered why. Was it possible that the Palmer marriage bed had not been a happy one?

She broke the silence by posing a question. 'Why are you suggesting that I should foster a ministry of my own?'

'All the information that I can find about your life indicates that you have loyally supported Scott in most of his endeavours. I cannot find any evidence that you have had your own plans or that any of them have ever been implemented. Scott's unexpected death could provide an opportunity to change this.'

This was a stab in the dark on Graeme's part, but he guessed it was correct and he wanted it to hit home hard.

'True,' said Pauline.

'Can I then suggest that you sell all of Scott's business ventures, either to his staff or his competitors, and then gradually begin a new life of your own that breaks new ground for the fostering of practical Christianity? My recommendation is that you keep half of the revenue to sustain a good life for yourself and put the other half into a charitable trust that funds God's work in innovative projects that you create far and wide.'

'Why give half of it away?'

'Why not? My basic understanding of your position is that you will have more than enough for your own needs and you will be spiritually empowered by your generosity.'

'Are you able to support this biblically?'

'Yes. Matthew, Chapter 6.'

'What does it say?'

'In summary, it says that if you make substantial gifts to people generously and privately, and seek no thanks or repayment, you will be blessed with new and plentiful spiritual power that you can use as you seek to achieve great things.'

'Have you practised this yourself?'

'Yes.'

'How?'

'Part of the royalties of my books go automatically into a charitable trust that does precisely this.'

'How should I use the spiritual power that I can receive by doing this?'

'By finding new and original ways to serve your God in the tradition that was begun by Scott, but you deliberately make your own by doing it differently.'

'Thank you. I will think about it.'

Graeme rose to go, and in doing so he issued an invitation to his farewell drinks. Her response was abrupt.

'Thank you. I will give it consideration.'

He left.

For the first time in weeks, Pauline had a feeling that her life was going to work out better than she had hoped it might.

Pauline was seated in the reception area of the offices of the Pentecostal Church, where Scott had been one of its powerful leaders for many years and she his most loyal supporter.

She was there to meet Timothy, who was standing in as chief pastor while the real one was serving his jail sentence for defying Covid-19 restrictions, the result of a practice of extremist religion that was now internationally infamous for causing the deaths of many members of the Church. Timothy also was the pastor whose role was to be the passionate advocate of the Prosperity Gospel, and he had been given the task by the congregation to sell it to the rest of the world as a matter of urgency. Scott had been his prime disciple.

Pauline was determined to get his advice and backing on how she could personally perpetuate Scott's mission to create many young prosperous Christians, but to do it her way. It was decision time. In her mind, it was just and right for her take over from Scott's mission. She had been the supporting actor for a long time, far too long in fact. But God had intervened.

Suddenly, Timothy arrived and greeted her warmly, inviting her into his office. 'Scott's funeral, though sadly small in attendance due to pandemic restrictions, was a wonderful tribute to him.'

'It was,' responded Pauline. 'Thank you for your appropriate words of praise for him.'

'It is never hard to honour a great man. I regarded it as a genuine privilege to have had a role in his farewell from our midst. May I add that your own words made a grand contribution to the occasion?'

'Timothy, I will value your advice on Scott's financial affairs and his legacy as a Christian.'

Thoughts began to generate quickly in Timothy's mind about the possibility of a significant financial legacy to the Church. He would encourage such thoughts with vigour.

'Go ahead,' he said.

While carefully appearing to seek advice, Pauline was clear in her mind as to what she wanted to do, and it was not that which Timothy was romancing.

'I want to sell all of the business interests that Scott has built up, with my help, over many years. I plan to invest half of it to sustain my life and personal interests. I have it in mind that the other half could go into a trust fund to help young Christians go into business and prosper. What do you think of that?'

'It sounds like a good plan to me. Could I suggest that you ask our Church to register and manage the trust, with you endowing it with the capital required?'

'No. I prefer to establish and control it myself, but I will be honoured if you will accept an invitation from me to be part of my team with the specific task of helping me find young Christians who want to go into business. I will pay you a director's fee for your time and a generous fee for every person you help me to sign up. It will be your decision as to how you use those fees in God's service.'

'It will be an honour. I humbly accept.'

He could easily recognise the obvious fact that it was God's clear intention that he should be personally prosperous.

'Can I also have your support,' Pauline said, 'in expressing my hope that we will place specific emphasis on encouraging Christian women to go into business?'

'I have no problems with that at all.'

'Thank you. I feel a special calling from God to significantly advance the cause of women. We have been ordinary servants for too long.'

'Agreed. Good thinking.'

'My initial planning is that the trust will make financial grants to not-for-profit companies pioneered by Christian women who live by the principles of the Prosperity Gospel. They will never have to pay us back. But they must, when they are operating at a surplus, be challenged to give that same amount of money to help another Christian who is starting a new not-for-profit company. In that way, our money keeps rolling over everywhere that we work.'

'I am baffled by your wish to have Christians establish not-for-profit companies. The Prosperity Gospel is quite clear in its teaching that making a profit is what God clearly wants his people to do.'

'The companies will make a profit, but there are no shareholders in this type of company. Everything is ploughed back into the business. All employees are paid top-quality salaries, but there are no bonuses for any of them.'

'I knew that Scott was advocating this enthusiastically, but I was unaware that he was promoting it exclusively.'

'He was not promoting it exclusively. I intend to do that.'

'May I ask why? It actually waters down the strength of the Prosperity Gospel when our calling is to ensure Christians have a good life and serve God mightily as a result.'

'It is a personal thing, Timothy. I want to make my own mark on God's world. Scott made his mark and did it well. Now I believe it's time for me to make mine, and I want to do it through the exclusive use of not-for-profit companies that meant so much to Scott.'

'But you are retreating from some very basic Christian principles that are the foundation of God's wishes that rewards are the right of the faithful.'

'No, I believe that not-for-profit companies are God's way of powerfully responding to the appalling ideology of socialists. We will create capitalists who work in a situation where everyone who is employed in the company shares in the profits. And we will also highlight the dominating role of women in these revolutionary companies. Socialists always claim that prosperous Christian capitalists treat women like slaves. I intend to disprove their allegation.'

'I am a little disappointed in the direction you are heading, Pauline, but I trust your integrity and will honour my commitment to work with you to make your plans a success. I wish you well in God's service.'

'Thank you. I will arrange a further appointment with you as soon as I have advanced the implementation of my plans.'

'God bless you, Pauline.'

'And you, Timothy.'

As he watched Pauline walk away, Timothy had a clear conviction that God would reward him for today's meeting.

'Good morning, Pauline, it's Graeme calling.' He had found Pauline's mobile number after a little devious research by some Christian friends. 'I know that you want to set up your own team for your trust fund and that you want to keep tight personal control, using people you can rely upon. I think that is wise. Can I suggest that you employ as your personal assistant a woman I know called Julia Hawke?'

Pauline did not enquire as to how Graeme had got her number, but she responded positively, saying, 'Give me her background.'

Graeme told her the full story of Julia, warts and all, including the training he was paying for to upskill as a law clerk. He made it clear that Julia had once been confused as to whether she liked girls more than boys, as this may prove to be a deal breaker. If so, he wanted to find this out now.

'She does not have the skills to manage your trust,' Graeme said. 'You need highly qualified professionals to do that. Her role can be looking after all your personal paperwork so that you can concentrate on the big picture. I can assure you that she is highly trustworthy. She has a deep need for a permanent and successful career. She will not mess up this opportunity to create stability in what has been a tumultuous life up to this point in time.'

'Ask her to call me.'

'I will.'

He breathed a sigh of relief that Julia's sexuality was not a deal breaker. Then he added, 'She was an atheist when I first met her, but seems to be turning away from that. Working for you may help her complete her journey. I don't think she will ever become a born-again Christian, but she can be convinced that Jesus of Nazareth is a person worth following.'

'I will keep that in mind.'

'Thank you.'

The conversation ended. There had been no warmth in it at all, just a slight acknowledgement that a working relationship was prospering.

Graeme sat at his desk at home and marvelled at what a great little old scout Jessie was. All this was her idea. It was a lucky night for Julia when Jessie had stumbled across her in the park. This raised in his mind the vexed issue of the theology of destiny, which he had rejected early in his career as a priest. But he was too weary to debate this matter right now.

Chapter Eighteen

The huge crowd had departed from Jamie's memorial service. To adhere to Covid-19 rules, it had been held in the open air at a local tennis stadium. There was lots of room that enabled adequate social distancing.

Graeme had given the eulogy every ounce of emotional energy that he had left in his tired frame, as he felt great affection for his departed friend. He was close to exhaustion, but he wanted a few private words with Annie. They found a secluded spot.

'Annie, may I say something very personal to you?' he asked.

'Of course, you can, Graeme.'

'I want you to fall in love once more.'

Annie was thunderstruck but remained silent.

'You loved your husband very much,' Graeme continued, 'and have spent decades of your life remaining faithful to him after his tragic death. You shared that love even more as you cared for Jamie magnificently, and did so happily. Now Jamie has departed. You, like me, are growing a little grey, but you have a couple of decades of love still in your soul. We must not waste it. In this city, there are many fine men of your age and character who live with loneliness. I want you to find one of them and let him experience your enormous capacity to love. You will find that he will return it in abundance.'

'I am lost for words.'

'I have run out of words, so just do it.'

'I have been wondering what my future life will hold. Sharing it with someone new may be a happy walk towards the sunset.'

'I am absolutely certain it will be. You were born to love. Now, may I also ask a favour of you?'

'Once more, the answer is yes.'

'There is a person in awful strife whom I am helping. Her name is Julia. The clothes she wears are just dreadful. If I introduce you to her, will you make her a couple of nice humble dresses and give them to her at no charge? She is dead broke.'

'Yes.'

He spent a few minutes telling her Julia's story. With every word that she heard she became happier to get involved.

'Sounds as though Julia needs a man in her life too.'

'A woman actually. And I think she may have found her, but you can let her sort that out.'

'Now, before you try to solve any more trials of humanity, you had better go home. You are close to konking out.'

'In just a moment, I will. But I want you to do one more thing for Julia. She needs help mentally as she is a self-wounded soul. Can you get her involved in the Mental Health Trust that Jamie established? It will point her in the right direction.'

'Of course.'

He scored a nice kiss for his efforts.

Chapter Nineteen

Penelope looked out at the school assembly of five hundred students and their teachers. She had called the assembly together at short notice to explain why she was taking one week of special leave in the mid-term for personal reasons. It was not the sort of message that could be handled well via email.

'Good morning,' she said. 'I have called you together today to confide to you a challenge that my family is experiencing at the moment, which will cause me to be absent from you for a week. My husband Graeme and I have been married for twenty-five years, and we have two children, Fiona and Luke, who are both twenty-two years of age. They are twins. Many of you have met all three, and they have been pleased to meet you.

Just a short time ago, Graeme was advised by a panel of eminent cancer specialists that he has cancers in several places in his body. The cancer cells are very aggressive and cannot be stopped. He was told that he would be dead within months, and that time is almost up.

At the time that Graeme heard their diagnosis, he made a decision that he would, at a time of his own choice, end his life by voluntary assisted dying, which as you know is legal in our nation when people have a terminal illness and decide to end their lives on a precise date that they determine. He made the required application to do so, and has gone through many interviews with doctors, psychiatrists and lawyers to verify that his illness is terminal and that he is of sound mind. Final legal approval has been granted, and Graeme, who is now in a rapidly declining state of health, will die tomorrow at 3pm at one of our city's hospitals. Tonight at 6pm, he will host drinks for an hour at our home with fifty of our family and friends to say goodbye in the happiest possible manner.

At sunset tomorrow, his ashes will be placed around a new tree that will be planted in a forest. Only Luke, Fiona and I will be present, along with Bishop Matthew Mark and the forestry workers. One week later, there will be a memorial service in the Anglican Cathedral conducted by the Bishop. I will return here immediately afterwards.

Fiona, Luke and I agree with and strongly endorse Graeme's decision to end his life by voluntary assisted dying. He goes to his death with complete faith in his God. He does not believe in life after death, and neither do I, though we respect those who do hold this belief.

Graeme hopes that his spirit will live on through the books he has written and which have been read by millions of people worldwide. I plan to continue my work here where we have a partnership to achieve excellence, trust and justice in a compassionate world. There is much that we can do together.

I greatly appreciate and value the friendship that you and I share. May grace and peace be with us all.'

Penelope moved to leave the stage but hesitated as everyone in the assembly rose to their feet. Spontaneously, the school captain came forward to the microphone. She had been given no notice of what Penelope would say, meaning she was totally unprepared in mind but filled with compassion for the highly respected leader of her college.

'Ms Penelope, may I say on behalf of every one of us here today that we love you dearly and respect you enormously. All of us will pray, in whatever way our religions provide, for you and your family, especially for Mr Brown. May God bless you and keep you among us for a long time.'

Quietly, Penelope said thank you and left the stage before she broke down.

The assembly remained standing. Tears flowed freely.

Chapter Twenty

The guests began to arrive for the farewell function that Graeme had described on the invitation as a 'Gathering of Eternal Friends'. Graeme had followed up his printed invitation with a phone call that explained, simply and carefully, the decision he had made about voluntary assisted dying and what date, time and place it would occur.

It was held at the spacious and comfortable home that he and Penelope had planned and built when his book sales reached generous heights. It was designed for the environment, generating all of its own power by sun and wind while controlling temperature solely through its design. They were conservative environmentalists. They had a large outdoor living area out among the flowers and the trees where guests would enjoy drinks and savouries. The weather was delightfully pleasant and the entire scene was a picture of peace.

It was nearing sunset on the final full day of his life, and nature had provided as beautiful a sunset as you could possibly hope for on such an occasion. He anticipated that the event would call on all his reserves of energy and emotion as his five deadly cancers were rapidly draining him. Nevertheless, he was ready to quietly turn on the finest and most humble performance of his life.

He had invited everyone to come at 6pm for an hour and had restricted the numbers to no more than fifty, including his family. Many had difficulty in making up their minds as to whether or not they had the courage to be there, even though they very much wanted to attend. But when the final roll call was made, no one had declined. There was a genuine air of respectful anticipation as to what might happen during this quite extraordinary hour of drinks.

It had been difficult to restrict the numbers to just fifty because through his high-profile public life and his caring attitude to the human race had accumulated many friends. But in the end, he made some hard decisions and left out some close mates to make way for some whom he had special reasons to invite.

The agenda was that his family, plus Aisha and her friend Dalai, would help him serve drinks and savouries. The choices included top-quality champagne, upmarket red and white wine, beer and a fruit punch. He would save his whisky for later in the evening. It tasted at its best when sipped quietly in a state of utter peace of mind.

While everyone was enjoying their drinks, he would have a personal chat to each attendant. Then he would close with a short speech, after which he would say his individual farewells before leaving the room. Those who wanted to stay on for a few minutes longer could do so if they wished, but it was anticipated that most would leave immediately.

———

Graeme, supported by a walking stick, placed himself near the door as he began his round of relaxed chats. His first one happened to be with Lyndon, who had served as Graeme's sole book publisher for more than two decades, and had masterminded the sales of millions of his seven books in almost every nation on the planet. They had a close working bond based on their strong mutual respect for each other's professional skills and their high regard for one another.

'Graeme, I have been tormenting myself for many long days about what words I would use when I met you at this unique party. Finally, I decided to say these truthful words. It has been a pleasure and a privilege to work with you for so many years. Together, we have put a great many wonderful words into the minds of thousands of readers. As the result, they have grown as people. You have given them many opportunities to foster life-changing thoughts that they can use to create a more humane and interesting society. Many have done just that. This has caused you and me to grow spiritually too, as well as financially. Thank you.'

'We have worked well together, Lyndon, and my dearest wish would be to spend many more years continuing to do just that. But it is not to be. Anyway, we have great memories. I treasure our friendship. Cheers.'

Lyndon had a further thought. 'I have in mind a project for our future too. I will mention it on the way out.'

'You said future.'

'I did.'

'Fascinating.'

—◆—

The funeral director was next.

'Hi, Bill,' Graeme said. 'Thanks for coming.'

'Thank you for inviting me, Graeme. I would not miss this for all the rice in China. Besides which, you are the most enthusiastic and reliable customer I have ever had. All paid up in advance, planned down to the finest detail and actually quite keen to go.'

'Well, I needed to make sure you would give me a send-off of the highest quality. We are not going to get any second chances with this.'

'Don't worry, I will make sure that this is organised better than a royal send-off, even though we won't have the Grenadier Guards performing. Can I also say this? You have changed my view of death. During my many years in this trade, I have always regarded death as death. An event that just had to happen. I now quite clearly see it as a very positive part of life, the last day in which we can happily cherish our friendships. It has taken me a long time to get the message, but I have got it.'

'It surely is.'

'You have caused me to work diligently on the whole philosophy of how my company organises and manages funerals. We must remove as much of the solemnity out of them as we can, and instead turn it into a process that helps people to accept that birth, life and death are a happy partnership of real value to every person.'

'I really do wish that I could be around to contribute to your mission with this.'

'Don't worry. You will be.'

'I surely will.'

———

A familiar figure appeared. The bishop.

'Blessings, Graeme. You are an extraordinary man. Quite unlike any other I have met. You have disturbed every theological bone in my body. But the experience has not been a bad one for me at all. My personal theology is experiencing some rethinking here and there, and I have a distinct feeling that the process will continue.'

'It means a lot to me that you have come tonight. Thank you, Matthew.'

'I understand that you will say a few words at the conclusion of our gathering tonight.'

'I will.'

'It is likely to further advance my theology, and so I await it with a good degree of anticipation. You must be under enormous strain as you face up to your final day tomorrow after having to talk pleasantly here tonight. Have you enough reserves in your tank to handle it all?'

'You may have difficulty in believing this, but I am actually on a high. This is the last party of my life. It has just got to be an absolute ripper.'

'Given your record of indomitable faith, I am certain that it will be.'

'I have a small task for you.'

'Ask and it shall be done.'

'Pauline Palmer will be here tonight, wife of Scott Palmer, who died of Covid-19.'

'The very public and heartfelt anger directed at the Palmers, as well as their pastor and their church, has been extraordinary but totally justified,' said Matthew. 'They represent the absolute pinnacle of human irresponsibility, and yet they call themselves Christians.'

'Because of that anger so volubly expressed by the community against her church,' replied Graeme, 'it is evident that her faith and her theology are in a fragile and volatile state. I can attest to this because I have personally experienced her wrath in recent days. She has been lashing out at everyone. However, there is hope that she may be gradually emerging from it. Her acceptance of my invitation to be here tonight is a step in the right direction, as I fully expected her to decline. I think that it may be helpful to her if she gets a word from you that tells her your door is always open if she ever feels the need to drop by for a chat about her future.'

'It may well test my patience and my capacity to forgive, but I will make it my business to do exactly that if the opportunity arises. I will let you know how it goes.'

Aisha arrived, escorted by Dalai. Aisha was a conservative person at heart who had radical thoughts on many issues of humanity that she exercised in a conservative manner.

Graeme was surprised, but in no way upset, that she was dressed in the trendiest clothing a Muslim woman could wear while still being adequately covered up. Even her hijab was of glamorous design and colour. It looked as though it came out of the latest Milan fashion show.

Aisha gave him a hug and a kiss on the cheek.

'You are looking even more beautiful than usual,' said Graeme.

'Thank you. This is a night of nights that I am not going to experience again. I felt compelled to dress appropriately.'

'You have achieved your goal.' He then chided Dalai. 'Why are you not decked out in the most upmarket Confucian gear?'

Dalai grinned broadly and said that the practice of the followers of Confucius was to share possessions. He would have been delighted to wear one of Graeme's suits had it been offered.

Graeme playfully told him that after 3pm tomorrow he was welcome to have any of Graeme's suits that he wished. He would mention it to Penelope.

'I have just checked,' Aisha said. 'All is set to go both legally and with the hospital tomorrow. There will be no legal hitches or organisational delays.'

'Your work for me in leading me through my end-of-life experience has been both efficient and compassionate and always helpful. I am hugely grateful.'

'I presume that your commitment to this choice of dying has not diminished in your final hours?'

'It has grown stronger.'

'I was sure it would have strengthened, but the law requires me to ask you once more. I am legally required to ask you again tomorrow before witnesses so you can sign yet one more document in your final minutes.'

'I know. You will once more hear my positive answer in a strong clear voice. My apologies, but now at this moment, I must ask you temporarily to move along. To my great surprise, my most difficult guest is about to arrive, and she has company. Would you mind chatting to Annie Glasgow and introducing her to a few people? I am not sure that she knows very many of tonight's guests.'

————

Three women came through the door together: Julia, Jessie and Pauline. Graeme was heartened that all three had formed some sort of a team, tenuous though it may be.

He received hugs from the first two and a formal, but no longer bitter, hello from the latter.

'It's great to see the three of you together,' said Graeme. 'Welcome.'

Jessie spoke on their behalf. 'We have only met in recent times and are just beginning an interesting journey together. We have taken a few initial steps with promising results and there will be more. Coming here tonight is one of the more important ones. Thank you for inviting us.'

Julia added, 'Your arrival in my life has created a revolution for me that I was certain would never be possible. I will never forget you. You are someone who is quite rare.'

'I am delighted that our paths have crossed,' was Graeme's sincere response.

Pauline knew that she needed to add something. 'I am pleased that you invited me to be here tonight,' she said.

Short, but it was a huge improvement on the tea-throwing episode.

With a smile, Jessie guided the other two inside. She was doing her Miss Marple thing very well as usual and enjoying every moment of it.

———

'Hello, Annie,' said Aisha. 'Lovely to see you here tonight so soon after Jamie's death.'

'Jamie would have wanted me to be here,' replied Annie. 'Graeme gave him very valuable help in making his decision to end his life in Switzerland and in helping him make all the arrangements with a hospital there. I wanted to be here tonight anyway. I am inspired by Graeme, and I find it to be an honour to be able to hear his final speech to the world. It will be a tremendous experience.'

'What has happened to Jamie's body?'

'I have arranged to have it flown back here. It just takes a long time to get all the necessary approvals from governments at both ends for reasons of community health and legal issues. There is a coroner's hearing in Switzerland that must certify that his death on the plane was from natural causes. We will bury him beside Mary. That is where he will want to be.'

'His death has reopened the debate on the extension of existing laws relating to voluntary assisted dying. The fundamental question now is this. Should VAD be confined only to people who are terminally ill, or should it be extended to cover older people who have simply had enough of life and genuinely want to go? Surveys show that there are far more people supporting Jamie's intention to end his long life than those who oppose it.'

'I intend to campaign to have our government allow people like Jamie decide to voluntarily die if they have no further reason to live. It will be a difficult battle to win politically, but it's one that must be won as it is decently humane. Every person is entitled to the right to decide whether they want to die or live on as a pitiful vegetable. The latter for some is a humiliation.'

'We can form a team on this one, Annie. I firmly believe we can win if we carefully enlist a formidable number of powerful allies to our side. Before tonight is over, you and I can organise what we can hope may be the first of many discussions with the bishop. We need him in our team.'

———————

Suddenly, there was a loud but cheerful noise at the door. Graeme went to investigate and was astonished to see The Donald advancing towards him.

'Thought I would surprise you. Had I advised anyone that I was attending, the news would have gotten around somehow and your street would have been blocked off by thousands of my irrepressible fans trying to tear my clothing off. So, here I am. I hope I won't be too much of an inconvenience by turning up in unexpected fashion.'

'You are most welcome, Donald. Come on in. My guests will be delighted to meet you in person and to realise that you have flown across the oceans to be here.'

'Came in my private jet. Lined up a couple of dinners here with my sponsors so I can claim it as a business expense. It's a big job keeping those guys happy.'

'This comment is not intended in any way to distract from my pleasure of welcoming you to my home tonight, but you did tell me during our interview on *The Donald At Large* that you were not impressed with suicidal people. Indeed, you made it fairly clear that you were quite allergic to us.'

'True. I said every word of it. But I can't get it out of my head that tomorrow you are determined to press a button that will instantly kill you while you have your family hold your hand. I said to myself that you must have something going for you that I am missing out on. I decided to take a last look at you on your final day and meet whatever friends come to your party. Maybe they are all crazy guys like you. Or maybe I am the nut. But I will never admit this on my broadcasts. So my only motive in being here is driven by fascination.'

'Please enjoy some happy research. Let me organise for one of my guests to introduce you around the entire gathering while I stay here to welcome more guests.'

Graeme thought quickly. Lyndon, the book publisher will be the one. He is an experienced man of the world who will relish this assignment. He beckoned to Lyndon who walked over to meet The Donald.

'Lyndon, meet my friend Donald Goldwater, whom you will recognise from *The Donald At Large*. Lyndon is my book publisher, Donald. Lyndon, would you introduce Donald to everyone in the room after first making sure he gets a drink?'

'Honour to meet you and take you on a meet and greet, Donald. Come this way.'

'Great to meet you, Lyndon. You must have made a packet as the publisher of Graeme's books.'

'I have.'

'So when he presses the button tomorrow, you will see a huge cash flow disappear.'

'I will.'

'Shouldn't you be talking him out of it?'

'That little exercise would keep him alive for another three weeks. He won't write another book in that time.'

With that comment, Lyndon quietly slotted away in his mind the thought that he might put in a major effort to sign up The Donald for a book.

———

There were many more guests steadily arriving. Graeme's lawyer was one and his accountant another. They would look after his estate and make life easier for Penelope, Luke and Fiona. They were competent and honest administrators of money. He trusted them and valued their presence.

His golf partner was also there. He took a golf ball from his pocket and asked Graeme if he would autograph it. His request was rewarded instantly.

Rabbi Jacob Isaacs arrived quietly. Graeme had a short chat with him, during which he mentioned that a Buddhist woman would arrive shortly and that he would like him to make her acquaintance as she needed a friend she could trust. Indeed, a short while later a young woman appeared wearing basic Buddhist clothing. Her arrival did bring one, quite audible gasp from the other side of the room.

Graeme stayed at the door welcoming the remainder of people while there was much animated chatter over drinks and nibbles, during which some notable dialogues took place.

———

Sarah had entered quietly and unannounced, enjoyed a quick but warm welcome from Graeme who was busily welcoming others, and then walked directly to where her mother Julia was standing. She gave her a kiss on the cheek and a light embrace.

'Hello, mother.'

'Oh, my goodness, Sarah. Hello. I am having enormous difficulty believing this.'

'So am I, but I am here.'

Julia began stammering in search for the right words. Jessie watched quietly as Julia said the wrong thing, just as Jessie had anticipated. 'How is it that you have been invited here to this almost unbelievable farewell party for a man who will die tomorrow, and why are you wearing such strange clothing?'

'I find it strange that you too have been invited,' replied Sarah. 'It does not seem to be your usual scene either. I was invited by Graeme Brown's children, Luke and Fiona. And my clothing indicates the fact that I am now a sincere and practising Buddhist, and I am wondering why your first words to me are ones that criticise me. You have not changed. It is just like the awful old days.'

'Oh dear, I do apologise. I am just struggling for words. I did not expect to meet you here. But please tell me. When and how did you meet Graeme's children?'

'Somehow Dr Aisha organised it.'

Jessie the Plotter looked on with admirable innocence.

'Why didn't someone tell me so I could have prepared myself?' asked Julia.

'Mother, does it really matter whether or not you knew what was happening in my life. You have to make a decision as to whether you are pleased to see me or not.'

Jessie entered the fray. 'Julia, you have retreated back into your sad old behaviour. You do not deserve to have a daughter.' Then she turned to Sarah. 'I am Julia's new friend. My name is Jessie. Can I say that I am delighted to meet you, even if Julia is not?'

Those words were clearly designed to hit Julia between the eyes, and they did.

'I did not mean to say any hurtful things,' said Julia. 'They just came out.'

Jessie's response was another thunderbolt. 'Then you should have remained silent. Please do for a while.'

Sarah calmed it down. 'Mother, I just want to say that I hope we can stay in touch from time to time, but live our separate lives with respect for one another.'

Julia was speechless for yet a few more moments, then said, 'I would like that.'

The conversation was cut short when the rabbi arrived on the scene. 'Could I introduce myself. I am Rabbi Jacob Isaacs. Our host, Graeme, for whom we all have well-earned respect, would like to meet Sarah. Could I interrupt?'

Sarah thought this was a fabulous idea, and so she walked away with the rabbi, thankful for the respite it gave her from Julia.

———

'Did Graeme Brown really ask to meet me?' enquired Sarah.

'Yes, he did. Dr Aisha has told him your story and he mentioned it to me. Graeme is a person who takes a genuine interest in how people acquire and live their faith. It's reflected in every one of the books he has written.'

At that moment, Graeme walked towards them and happily greeted Sarah. 'Thank you for coming along tonight, Sarah. My apologies for being a bit tied up when you arrived. Aisha has told me interesting and inspiring things about your life, as have Fiona and Luke. May I also say that if I was handing out a prize for the most noticeable person in the room, you would win easily?'

'Thank you. I wear traditional Buddhist clothing always. There are some adornments that can be added, but I have no interest in them. Nor do I ever wear make-up. However, I do take time to ensure that my hair looks well cared for.'

'It does, and you have helped make this gathering an ecumenical occasion. In addition to you, we have your escort of this moment, Rabbi Jacob, eminently representing the Jewish faith. Over there, as you can see, we have Dr Aisha from the Islamic community and her friend Dalai, who is involved with Confucianism. And we have your mother too, who is an atheist. She won't agree that atheists are religious, but they are. Now, can I enquire as to why you chose to become a Buddhist? I became a Christian simply because I was born into a Christian family. They were Presbyterian, but I became an Anglican. Right now, in my heart, I am a Pilgrim. I am interested to hear of your faith journey.'

'My life has always been unstable and uncertain,' said Sarah, 'so I sought a faith that would help me handle this. Buddhists believe that we live in an ever-changing world, and we are best able to handle this by constantly striving to achieve enlightenment. I have set out on that pathway. Clearly, I have a long journey ahead of me if I am to become an enlightened person. I believe it is worth the best shot I can give it.'

Rabbi Jacob contributed a helpful comment. 'My experience of religious life is that we all need a cornerstone around which to base our lives, and I found that in God and the Prophets. I admire Buddhists, but it always seemed to me that the only cornerstone of your faith is the self-discipline you impose on yourself. In fact, you must become selfless. This must put real pressure on you as you go on your journey.'

'It does, but it also challenges me to be a stronger person, and I enjoy that challenge.'

'I admire you for that Sarah,' continued Graeme. 'I have rejected the creeds and dogmas of my Church primarily because of their negativity, but my spiritual strength comes from being a Pilgrim who walks the paths of life in company with a giant of a man called Jesus of Nazareth, who gives me strength. Except for the Jesus factor, we are not far apart.'

'Jesus is a man who interests me as a role model, but I switched off from Christianity early in my life as my mother, Julia, was always threatening me that she would tell God how awful I was and that God would punish me. Years later, when she told me she was not a Christian, I asked her why she had always threatened me with the wrath of God. She said that she thought it was a good way to keep me in order. I still see Christianity as being very negative, and I want to give Buddhism a really good try. I hope that I can stay with it for the long term. If I fail, it will not be for the want of trying.'

Graeme found some appropriate words to bring all these good thoughts together. 'I will be with you in spirit, Sarah.'

'Sarah,' Rabbi Jacob added, 'here is my card with my mobile and private email address. If ever you need a friend or simply someone to talk to, I will answer, gladly and helpfully.'

'I love you both,' Sarah answered sincerely. Then she saw Fiona and Luke beckoning her and politely excused herself as she moved in their direction. Graeme thought this to be an opportune time to have a frank conversation with Julia and Jessie, while Jacob headed in the direction of Penelope.

'Good evening, Penelope,' said Rabbi Jacob. 'We meet again in what are very challenging days for you. And if I can say so, I find them to be an experience that leads me to an opening to a different world.'

'Greetings to you, Jacob,' replied Penelope.

'My spies at Abraham College tell me that you brought tears to the eyes of many with your speech today in which you told them about Graeme's death tomorrow. I have listened to it online, and I must say that I was greatly moved spiritually by your simple but compassionate words.'

'It means much to me, Jacob, to hear you say this. I was not confident that my words were the best that I could have used, nor did I feel that I delivered them in the way that I hoped. I sincerely wanted to handle it well, and I hoped that, if I stumbled, my audience would understand.'

'All speeches have defects in them. Even Winston Churchill felt that his best speeches were his worst. I knew as I watched that you were under pressure, and I want to say that I yearned to take some pressure from you, but no one could have done that. Tell me, how do you live with a person who has planned his death to the very last day and precise moment?'

'It has been much easier than I thought. This is because Graeme has gone out of his way to make it as comfortable as possible for me, Fiona and Luke.'

'How did he do that?'

'It all happened steadily and progressively, but the crucial occasion was when the four of us sat around the dinner table one night and agreed on the date of Graeme's death, so that we could accept that he was going at that time. Then we worked out what were the essential things to be done to ensure that Graeme was ready to go. For example, we went into as much detail as we could about all the crucial matters. These included the legal requirements of voluntary assisted dying, matters pertaining to the distribution of his estate, what would happen to his personal possessions, which people should know about his planned death, who we should personally visit to say goodbye, how we would organise this party, who should be here, and what we should all do on the day of his death. Finally, we decided that he should try to do a few good deeds to help people who had problems, so that he was spiritually productive right to the end. We suddenly became aware of the time we had taken to discuss all these matters. It was midnight and we had not noticed.'

'Did you all feel totally drained at midnight?'

'No, not at all. We were all determined to make this time the finest three months of our lives. And it has been.'

'I am uplifted by that, Penelope. Thank you for sharing it. May God add to your strength.'

———

It was one of those occasions that often happen at social functions. There was a moment when Bishop Matthew found himself left alone in the middle of the room with someone he had not met before. He quickly realised that it was Pauline Palmer and welcomed the opportunity to meet with her, as had been suggested by Graeme.

'May I share your company for a while?' he asked. 'My name is Matthew. I am the local Anglican bishop, and I assume that you are Pauline Palmer?'

She responded warmly. 'I am. Good evening, Bishop.'

Matthew opened the discussion with appropriate comments, sincerely held, about Scott's death. Then he commented, 'I have no right to probe into your private affairs, but may I ask what you now plan to do in your future life? In the now-expanded scale of longevity, you are still a young person.'

'Thank you for that comment. I believe exactly what you say, but so many people enquire as to how I intend to spend my retirement years. So I tell them that I have no intention of ever retiring.'

'Good for you. What interesting ventures do you plan to undertake in the many years that lie ahead of you?'

'Actually, I will be grateful for your advice on my plans. May I say to you confidentially that I intend to sell every business that Scott had owned, and, after leaving adequate funds to allow me to live comfortably and to travel wherever I wish, I will set up a trust that will enable me to encourage young Christians, particularly women, to create not-for-profit companies that enhance the expansion of a positive Christian world.'

Pauline went on to explain the concept of not-for-profit companies, then outlined her vision of how the role of women will be to provide frontline leadership in the entire venture. The bishop was more than a little impressed by what he had just heard.

'Is this a vision that will highlight what your husband achieved in his life's work?'

'In part, yes. But it will be my creation. I loved my husband and we spent our entire life together loyally and enthusiastically backing his dreams. Now that he has gone, I want to be my own person and take his initial vision regarding not-for-profit companies into a far broader realm than what he envisaged.'

'Do you see it as your Christian calling?'

'No.'

'May I ask why not?'

'It is designed to promote Christianity as a force that spreads wealth among as many as is possible in the world of business, but I do not believe that God designed it. I have created it because I am fired with spiritual power.'

'You have made a number of comments that are worthy of wider discussion, and I would welcome the opportunity to take part in that. Rest assured that I will keep your comments confidential. I wish you well. Can I also ask a favour? If I find young Christian women who want to go into business in a way that serves the community, so they can leave a mark on society, may I introduce them to you?'

'Yes. Please do and do it often.'

'Thank you. I wish you well, Pauline. Please stay in touch.'

Bishop Matthew discovered that he was not about to be spared from another enlightening chat. Annie and Aisha stood in his way, a fact that did not appear to worry him.

'Good evening, Bishop. Can you spare a moment to talk with two women who have a crusading mission on their minds?' said Annie.

'The Lord himself has throughout history sent us divine commands to be missionaries at all times,' replied the Bishop. 'So how could I avoid such a discussion with you?'

Aisha and Annie introduced themselves and outlined their relationship with, and total support of, the life and death decisions of both Graeme and Jamie. They carefully explained that they intended to put intense pressure on the politicians of the nation to extend voluntary assisted dying laws, so as to allow older people to legally take the step that Jamie had attempted, and to not have to travel to Switzerland to achieve it.

With hope in her voice, Annie said, 'Bishop Matthew, we would welcome you as one of the leaders of our team.'

Bishop Matthew took a deep breath and looked to the heavens for help. He saw only a roof that locked him in. 'I am used to hearing confessions,' he said, 'not making them, so let me first confess that Graeme's decision to end his life by using VAD laws shook me to the theological core. However, I am firming towards the belief that he has a right of choice to do it, and that I have a right of choice not to. This is helped by the fact that he is dying quickly, so we are not creating a death, we are just bringing forth the inevitable. Now, in the case of Jamie, his death was some way off, as he was in good shape for a centenarian. His decision was close to being clearly described as suicide. I have significant problems with that.'

Aisha handled this one. 'Jamie was in good shape for a person of his age,' she said, 'but his arthritis was worsening fast and he had the first signs of Parkinson's. Soon he would have been spending years in bed. After one hundred active years of considerable achievement, he had earned the right to avoid that. He held no fear of death, but he found the prospect of living as a vegetable to be completely offensive.'

Annie bought into the debate. 'Bishop Mark, there are several valid reasons why Jamie chose the path he took. One was that Mary was the love of his life. She took her own life decades ago, but he kept her as a cornerstone of his life for all those years. He recently reached a point where he wanted to join her. Unlike Graeme, Jamie passionately believed in life after his death. Graeme respected him for that and made no effort whatsoever to change his mind on it.

Jamie fervently wanted to be with Mary, and he believed that if he arranged to end his life in a manner somewhat similar to her, he would go to the same place in eternity as Mary. The difference was that he was doing it in a civilised way, whereas her death was quite violent. Can you condemn a committed Christian like Jamie for seeking eternal life a little earlier than may have been God's will?'

'We are beginning a debate that will tear my Church apart in bitter acrimony.'

'Bishop,' said Annie, 'with all the respect that I can muster, it does not matter to the cause of humanity if your Church tears itself apart. What is at issue is this. Christians spend their lives preparing to go to Heaven and pray constantly that when their time comes, God will let them in. But they get nasty when offered a chance to get there early. They go to extremes to avoid it. This is hypocrisy. If they are sincere, they should be trampling over one another in their haste to get to Heaven.'

'You have placed before me some very difficult questions, and I sense that you will never let me off the hook on any of them.'

'It is not a matter of letting you on or off the hook about anything. We are just asking you for an honest debate within your Church about these issues. May we ask that at the next synod of your diocese, you hold a public forum on the expansion of VAD laws? We would welcome the opportunity to speak and debate, and hope that people who oppose us will get equal time. The result of the forum can then be conveyed to government.'

'How can I with any integrity deny your request? With a heavy heart, I will do it. There will be many who'll praise my decision to hold it, and many who'll condemn me. May God have mercy on my soul and theirs.'

'We believe that He will,' said Annie.

———————

'You look as though you are enjoying yourself, Jessie,' said Graeme. He thought that Jessie and Julia were looking more than a bit aggravated with one another, so had decided to add a few words that might lighten up the conversation.

Jessie got the spirit of the message. 'I am,' she responded. 'In all my years I have never been at such a wonderful party in such a lovely home where I could drink such splendid red wine and enjoy exotic savouries such as I never believed existed. If it was in different circumstances, I would say, "Please, invite me often."'

'How about you, Julia, do you feel the same way?'

Julia was unable to join in Graeme's efforts to lighten up the conversation. 'I am trying to restore my equilibrium,' she said. 'I have just met and spoken with my daughter, Sarah, for the first time in three years.'

'Was this good or bad? I hope it was the former.'

'It should have been good, but I was shaken to the core by the unexpected surprise. It put me in a state of panic and I said all the wrong things. So much so that Jessie has been scolding me for being stupid and selfish.'

'This is more than a little sad. Do you want to rebuild your relationship with Sarah or will it cease again tonight? I would like to suggest that the rebuilding process should now be steady. What do you think, Jessie?'

'I am sure that you are right. An emotional get together immediately after this could end in disaster, as too much bad blood has flowed under the bridge for too many years and tonight's words from Julia have not helped, particularly as Sarah made a genuine attempt to re-establish their relationship. Julia has lived for forty unhappy years and needs to come out of them steadily and very slowly to create a stable existence for herself.'

'What is your reaction to this, Julia?'

'I did handle this badly tonight, and I think that the task of rebuilding my life in a way that includes Sarah is the right way to go.'

'May I first make a hard-hitting comment to you?' said Graeme. 'As I see it, your life has been a selfish one. You have always seen the world as your enemy and consistently acted in self-defence. It is a basic task of personal reform that you must work at consistently. This is shown by the fact that your first reaction tonight was to protect yourself, not giving one moment's thought to the huge effort that Sarah made in coming here tonight. You should be thoroughly ashamed of yourself.'

Julia could do nothing but avoid his eyes and look intently at the floor.

Graeme offered a solution. 'I can see by your reaction that you are feeling sorry for yourself again. Let me tell you a true story that will help you snap out of it.' Graeme then told her a story of a seventy-five-year-old woman who had served as a warden in a parish church where Graeme was rector.

On one Christmas Eve, after helping him conduct a carol service, she walked home and was brutally attacked and raped by a seventeen-year-old youth. He was eventually caught and charged. At the trial, when she was called to give evidence, she told the judge that she bore no malice towards her attacker. She felt very sorry that he was in such a bad mental state that he committed acts of violence, and asked the judge to be lenient in whatever sentence was needed to rehabilitate him.

'May I suggest that you get a heavy dose of that quality of forgiveness into your attitude towards all whom you feel have hurt you in some way?

Additionally, share some kind words with Sarah on your way out this evening and agree to a further meeting sometime. It will be a good start, Julia, if you talk earnestly to Sarah about her Buddhist faith and learn from her one of its fundamental principles of the pathway to enlightenment. It is this. You must detach yourself from yourself. Think about it hard.

Having now finished my sermons, let me say that I rejoice in the positive news that Pauline Palmer is giving you some work for a month helping her sort out her legal issues, as distinct from those concerned with her late husband's companies. I hope that you can make it permanent so that you never again go to a park with a knife.'

Julia walked towards him and took hold of his hands, looking into his face in a way that sought forgiveness. He kissed her cheek and reached out to hold Jessie's hand too.

'Jessie, may I say that you have been a wonderful friend to Julia? Particularly as you had never met until you accidentally stumbled across her in the park. I am delighted that the paths of all three of us have crossed. You will keep opening doors for Julia, won't you?'

'I will certainly do my best to do so, and will add a few regular kicks in the pants too, whenever she slips back into her dark days. You are the first man of God I have ever trusted. You talk sense, and it is just so unchristian for anyone to talk sense. It's a great pity that you are not going to be around to talk more sense to the pompous and pious who flock to churches.'

Julia finished the discourse. 'Both of you have given me a clear ray of hope. I can build my new life on the hope that I can improve my personal discipline and relationships as well as make loving contributions to Sarah's life. I am blessed by our friendship.'

'Goodness me,' said Jessie. 'You actually used a Christian word. Blessed. This is getting dangerous.'

———

Dalai decided to cease being a passive bystander and reckoned that a conversation with the bishop might be an opportunity to leave a mark on the evening.

'Your Grace,' said Dalai, 'may I interrupt you for a moment? My name is Dalai. I am a close friend of Dr Aisha Jinnah, who is Graeme's doctor.'

'Thank you for making yourself known to me, Dalai. It will be good to get to know you personally. Please call me Matthew.'

'This is a privilege for me, Matthew. I am a follower of Confucius and I am a migrant who came here from China, specifically from the island of Hainan.'

'Well, this is interesting, Dalai. You are the first follower of Confucius I have ever met.'

'I do hope that I will not be the last. Could I ask for the honour of meeting with you soon at your office to discuss the possibility of creating a study link between Christians and Confucians?'

'Yes. It certainly is possible. Let me give you my card with my contact details. I will alert my PA that you will be calling to make an appointment. Broadly speaking, what are the areas of life that you feel could be common ground for Confucians and Christians?'

'I think that it would be good for us to try to more fully understand what we all believe. I hope that I am wrong, but I have always held the view that Christianity promotes selfishness. Christians strongly emphasise forgiveness of personal sins and an assurance that one day you will go to Heaven and enjoy an eternal life denied to non-believers. In a world of personal greed, this does not seem a good space to occupy. On the other hand, Confucians are poor at explaining ourselves. Most of those who study our beliefs feel that the importance of sharing, which we emphasise in our lives, is impractical and will never work. They see us as being silly dreamers.'

'I will welcome a discussion about all of your comments. Tell me, what are the beliefs of a Confucian, beyond sharing?'

'Before I answer that, may I further emphasise our misunderstanding about sharing? Mao Zedong took advantage of it when he used it as a means of gaining power in China in 1948. He pretended that he was a Confucian and that communism would help create a Confucian world of sharing. He deceived millions of Chinese, as he had no intention of ever sharing anything. Mao simply understood the crucial steps necessary to gain political power, and he was determined to have it totally, so he enticed Confucians to back him.

Beyond that, we seek wisdom, discipline and piety, and we have no fear of death. We constantly remind our followers that death is a great event in our lives. This is one reason why I greatly admire Graeme. He is facing death in a very Confucian manner. You will note when I attend Graeme's memorial service that I will wear white. Every Confucian wears white at a funeral. Never black. It is not a time of mourning.'

'Our discussion will be an enlightening one. Beyond our meeting, what are you seeking in the long term?'

'I will proceed slowly. When Penelope has resumed her work at the College of Abraham, I will seek a meeting with her. Confucianism is not a part of college life at present. But I hope we can become positive partners of hers, as a fundamental element of following Confucius is the constant accumulation of knowledge.'

'Perhaps I can help with that. Let's start a journey. It could well be a significant one as there can be no doubt that Confucius is regarded in both academic and religious circles as one of the most significant people in the history of humanity, his influence reaching far beyond China.'

'We will, and thank you. I hope we can decide as we travel together whether Confucianism is a religion or a secular morality.'

Graeme put aside his walking stick and sat on a comfortable chair to address his friends in his final public speech. Some also found seats, others chose to stand. Silence descended upon the gathering. There was a genuine presence of electricity in the gathering, and all were alert in a huge moment of expectation.

'My friends, the time has come to say goodbye. All too early.

'Just before he died, Renoir said to his wife, "The sad thing is that I am only just beginning to understand the basics of art." I am in exactly the same position as Renoir, except that I am not an artist. Nevertheless, I have my greatest book ready to be written, and I have it planned in my mind. But it is not to be, even though all my books have been a basic training ground for this one.

'You are aware from reading my books and hearing my speeches that I do not believe in life after death or in Heaven or Hell, but I respect your right to believe in them if you do. I believe in death after life, as I am certain that when I die, I am dead forever. So, we will not meet again.

'My body will soon be ashes and dust, and that's the best fate for it, rather than it being in its current cancerous state of uselessness.

'You will eventually find my remains resting around a new tree that will add to the natural life and beauty of our nearby national park. However, cancer will never kill my spirit. It will become part of the life of that tree and will remain there long after I am forgotten.

'How long will it take for me to fade from memory? Who knows, but I hope that my legacy will be of some use to humanity in the years that lie ahead, but I will not be in a position to worry if it is shorter rather than longer. I will be at peace.

'You are welcome to drop by the tree once in a while. It won't be marked by a plaque or a cairn. Penelope will tell you exactly where it is if you ask her nicely. But please don't try to talk to me there. I would prefer that we just meditate quietly together as you sit beside the tree. My most fervent hope is that my spirit will be in communion with your living spirit and may nourish your life in some way.

'I love you all, and that love will never die even though I will. Go from here now with no sadness in your hearts. This has been a happy hour that I have cherished mightily. It is part of our journey together to the rim of eternity. You will all reach the rim at different times in the years ahead. As you travel there, may your faith grow and be with every one of you forever.'

There was no applause. It would have been absolutely inappropriate. There was a wonderfully warm feeling in the hearts of all. Most would be at a loss to describe it.

Quietly, his friends put down their drinks and gradually formed appropriately small departure queues, which had orderly physical distancing, as they chatted among themselves about Graeme's departure speech while waiting to say a final goodbye to him. Many asked one another for guidance about what would be the most appropriate words to convey to him.

Most were speechless or very close to it. Many broke Covid-19 rules to give him a warm handshake or a big hug, and most spoke only a few halting but very sincere words.

Nevertheless, a few had something to say, and their words were memorable.

———

While they were lining up, Barton Deakin assailed The Donald. All evening he had been waiting for an opportunity to arise after having quickly greeted Goldwater a little earlier when the talking legend was being introduced around the room.

'May I reintroduce myself? My name is Barton Deakin. I want to ask why you are so frightened of dying that you have to lash out and demean decent people like Graeme Brown, who has no fear of death.'

'I beg your pardon?'

'I watched you with absolute disgust while you grossly insulted our host Graeme on your program. You accused him before millions of listeners of planning to commit the crime of suicide, when you knew perfectly well that he had no such intention. He was about to participate in voluntary assisted dying, which is legal throughout our nation. You did it because you are petrified at the thought of dying yourself and are frightened that one day your own family will put you away with a needle because they are appalled by your constant denigration of people. Of course, the VAD laws won't allow your family to do that to you, but you are too frightened to trust anyone. So you lash out at Graeme in the crudest possible fashion. How low is it possible for you to get?'

Barton had made a lethal, predetermined statement aimed at getting an aggravated response.

'Could I say, loudly and clearly,' said The Donald, 'that I don't give a stuff what you say or think about anything? Get out of my way.'

Barton stood his ground. 'That is the only truthful statement you have made in your entire life. You do not give a stuff about anyone or anything except Number One, and you so lack confidence in yourself that you have cooked up this silly little talk show to convince yourself that you are a great man who has built up a huge listening audience, who are dumber than you are, if that is possible. You could not possibly take the risk of talking to anyone with brains.'

'I am about to punch your face in.'

'You would not have the guts to try. There are very few people in the world that I can beat in a punch up, but you are one of them. I invite you to try right now.'

'Who in hell are you?'

'I have told you my name. I work at the university.'

'Given your arrogance, you must be one of the bouncers.'

'In a way I am. I do have powers to kick out a few troublesome students.'

'What is your exact job?'

'I lecture in law.'

'At your age, you should have risen higher than a lecturer. You have obviously stuffed up your career.'

'I should have done better and became the boss of the whole university, but I settled for second best. I am just the Dean of the Faculty of Law. But I did get doctorates at both Oxford and Harvard, so I haven't done too badly. Before I took up my university career, I was a barrister of the Supreme Court. Made a bit of a name for myself winning a few high-profile defamation cases against media companies. I am itching to take up a case again just to keep my hand in. Graeme would be a real good client to have. I would appear for him at no charge.'

'Don't threaten me.'

'Did not think I did. I just answered your question.'

'What is it exactly that you are trying to achieve by this confrontation?'

'When you report to your dumb listeners about how you really enjoyed Graeme's final party, could I suggest that you humbly admit that you misjudged Graeme? Tell them you apologised to him on the way out today. Just as importantly, you could suggest to them that if they wind up in Graeme's situation, they should take a good look at what he has done and make an objective choice instead of listening to windbags like you.'

'I will consider it.'

'Don't tax your brain too much.'

With that, they parted company in silence. Barton knew that he had overstepped the mark, but he was certain it was the only language that The Donald would understand. He handed out worse than that on most of his programs.

Nevertheless, Barton knew that he deserved to be put in the naughty corner.

———

Annie Glasgow was first to embrace him.

'I want to ask you a favour, Graeme,' she said.

'Certainly.'

'Say hello to Jamie for me tomorrow afternoon?'

'I will be with him in spirit.'

'Do you think he will have found Mary?'

'She will be wherever his spirit is. They are a team.'

'You can be assured that at 3pm tomorrow. I will be with you in spirit. We are part of a beautiful team that is called hope.'

'We most certainly are.'

'I am now going to tell you something very personal.'

'I am intrigued.'

'I am going directly from here to the Playhouse Theatre, where I will meet a new friend who has invited me to a play followed by supper.'

'This friend is male?'

'Yes.'

'Wow! How did you meet him?'

'Many years ago, when my husband Robert and his brother James were killed in a road accident. The young police officer who came to tell me the tragic news is my escort tonight. His name is Sean Murphy. A few months later, he was the policeman who came to tell me that my mother-in-law, Mary, had driven her car over a cliff. I went with him to tell Jamie.

He rose through the police ranks to become chief inspector. A year ago, his wife died. She had severe dementia for three years. I met him occasionally when he came to seminars organised by the Mary Glasgow Mental Health Trust.

Just yesterday, he phoned to say he had two theatre tickets and he invited me to join him. I found myself instantly agreeing, as it almost seemed as though you had sent a spiritual message to him through the heavens.'

'Well, I can assure you that you have been much in my thoughts. To me, you represent genuine life and love.'

'I hope that I do. And you will laugh when you hear this. The show at the theatre tonight is *Annie Get Your Gun*.'

'For goodness sake, don't get your gun. Just surrender.'

———

Lyndon the book publisher was in a determined frame of mind when he spoke to Graeme.

'I will search the world to find an author who has talent somewhere near your skill with words and your expansive theology,' said Lyndon 'Someone willing to write a great novel based on your life, beliefs and courage, as well as the low points of your life, so readers can personally relate to you. I reckon it can be called *A Beautiful Sunset*, and I will work tirelessly to make sure that it creates a new Reformation of considerably significant scope. It's long overdue, five hundred years in fact, and the time is right. For me it will be an act of love.'

'I greatly appreciate and value your sincere offer, Lyndon. But can I suggest that you won't have to look far in your quest to find the right author? Penelope has plans to become an author of quality in her own right, and she hopes to begin her new life by writing my story. As you know, she is a very talented person who admits openly that she will need a lot of professional help. She would gain enormous confidence if she could have you as her mentor and implementer with this. She will be a considerable asset, as she knows me better than any other person on the planet.'

'What wonderful news this is. I will meet with her soon. Consider it done. In fact, it is a greater certainty than the fact that the sun will come up tomorrow morning.'

'You bring me much happiness.'

'I just hope that out there, somewhere in the spirit world, you will be able to keep writing books.'

As he approached Graeme, Bishop Matthew was close to tears.

'You are a wonderful and faithful servant of our Lord, Graeme. It is now clear to me that I should have tried to gain an understanding of your theology many years sooner than I have done now. May your spirit live on in the hearts of many. It will have an important place in my life and in my heart. Travel safely, good friend.'

'Matthew,' responded Graeme, 'my recent times of dialogue with you have been of real spiritual value to me. I am grateful for your openness and your goodwill. How did you get on with Pauline Palmer?'

'Quite pleasantly actually. She is determined that she will make a much greater impact on the world than her husband ever dreamed of achieving, and she will do it her way, turning it into an powerful feminist movement as she moves forward. The promotion of not-for-profit corporations represents a refreshing change from pure capitalism, and her plan to have it acknowledged as a female initiative is worth a try. We have had too many male initiatives dominating the world for too many centuries. Her greatest hurdle is her personality and style. She has rigid views and an uncompromising way of communicating. These have the potential to destroy her. Even so, I hope she gets there. She welcomed my invitation to meet occasionally, but did not suggest an immediate meeting.'

'Well done, this is a step forward.'

'Graeme, may I add that your influence on me has spread far beyond our personal relationship? I have just had a challenging but enlightening conversation with Annie Glasgow. What a fine human being she is. She has shaken me considerably with her plan to broaden the scope of voluntary assisted dying to an even greater extent than you have. As you will already know, her father-in-law, Jamie, was an old dyed-in-the-wool Presbyterian traditionalist. He passionately believed in life after death and was on his way to Switzerland to end his life just because he had had enough of it. He wanted out so he could be with his wife, who had taken her own life years ago. And Annie agreed with him one hundred per cent. These are devout Christian people.'

'What do you plan to do about it, Matthew?'

'I was strongly of a mind to dismiss her aims as impossible, but Aisha Jinnah joined in and backed her strongly, so I agreed to hold a public forum on VAD at our Anglican synod. I will participate with an open mind. I don't know if I am doing the right thing, but I could think of no valid reason to sweep the issue under the table. I have to face the fact that my attitude to VAD, and that of my Church, may be wrong. I need to find an answer to this as soon as I can.'

'There will always be two points of view about VAD, Matthew. Your job is to make sure that both are recognised as human rights. You have made a wise and brave start on an inevitable journey.'

'I do sincerely hope that I have.'

'May we both follow the same pathway as Jesus of Nazareth in creating a better world.'

As he walked away, the bishop had a spring in his step. Graeme actually hoped that he could, in spirit, be in the team with him at the public forum on VAD. Now that he came to think of it, Dalai the Confucianist could join in too.

Bill, the funeral director, had no tears in his eyes, but he was clearly deeply moved by the occasion and wished that he did not have to leave.

'Have no words that would grace this incredible occasion, my friend, so I won't even try. I will say a sincere farewell. I want you to know that I wish that I could be with you on your journey tomorrow, but I accept that my role is simply to open a door for you.'

'I reciprocate your thoughts,' responded Graeme, 'and express the hope that you continue to help people die well and grieve positively.'

'Vale, my friend. I most surely doubt that I will ever meet another like you.'

Pauline Palmer was next. She gave Graeme a kindly look that could be described as neither warm nor cold, but at least it was open. Whatever her state of mind, she nevertheless had words to say that struck a chord far sweeter than on previous occasions, even though she made no attempt to express any sorrow about her efforts to wound him with hot tea. She spoke without emotion and with no animation on her face.

'You and I are a long way apart in our Christian beliefs, but the gap is not as far distant as it used to be or needed to be. Your spiritual strength is very deep indeed, and your courage can only be described as astonishing. I am very sad that Scott was not able to die in the state of peace that you are about to experience tomorrow, but there is little that we can do about it now. Be this as it may, I will strive to experience at least some of your peace as my own life continues. Especially, I will stop to think of you at 3pm tomorrow. There won't be tears in my eyes, but there will be some hope in my heart. I bid you farewell.'

Graeme would have preferred to say that an apology would have been a fond farewell, but felt there was a need to say something with kindness.

'I am pleased, Pauline, that we have shared some time together in recent days. I have come to understand your Christian journey, and I have grown as a result. I wish you well in your new endeavours.'

Next up was Julia. 'You have taught me the difference between an honourable death and a cowardly one,' she said to Graeme. 'You have also revealed to me what a good life can be like. I will never reach your quality of life, but I am going to strive to head in your direction and put a big effort into my attempt to live well and to learn to love others, especially my daughter. Your wise and direct comments tonight have jolted me out of my past in a very practical way. This means that when my death arrives on the radar, I will be ready to die well, and I hope that my spirit might help others even if it's just a tiny reflection of what you are doing. I cherish you as a wonderful brother, Graeme.'

'I share your goodwill, Julia. May you grow in spiritual strength and may your best days lie ahead of you.'

Jessie followed. 'It is a huge pity that I did not marry you instead of the irresponsible creep that I did. But it is no good crying over spilt milk, is it? Clearly, I haven't got too many years left, but you are a shining light for whatever my limited future is. I am going out there to try to kick one or two more good goals for the human race before my arthritis takes over. And you never know, I might find an old bloke a bit like you to keep me company. You have convinced me that it is worth a try. Miracles happen.'

'In normal circumstances, Jessie, I would put big money on you to kick goals and to find a good mate. Nevertheless, meeting you has been a joy. You have brought light to my fading days.'

Sarah began to leave with them, a sight that delighted Graeme. She and Julia seemed to be establishing a tentative connection. But before she left, she had some uplifting words to say.

'My meeting with Fiona and Luke in the park, where Julia tried and failed to end her life, was a wonderful day in my life. They followed it up with a warm welcome earlier tonight. I find them to be beautiful people, and they learned how to be beautiful people from their father and mother. I had the privilege of meeting Penelope too. She is an inspiring person.'

'I agree totally with your comments about my family. But I had little to do with them becoming fine people. They became fine human beings quite naturally.'

'Your attitude to your death tomorrow is something that Buddhists would regard as a true state of enlightenment. I believe that your spirit will return to the earth in the same model as you have created by your compassionate presence.'

'That would be wonderful.'

'I love you dearly.'

'You are loved by me too, and I hope that someday you and Julia will acquire mutual respect that may then grow closer.'

'Farewell, good man.'

———

Rabbi Jacob was upbeat. He sensed that his final conversation with Graeme must not have one moment of sadness.

'Graeme, a sacred moment in the long history of the Jewish people is the time when Moses led them out of bondage in Egypt and took them on a long journey to the promised land of Israel. On the way he parted the Red Sea, drowning the Egyptian Army that pursued him. Then he made a fateful decision to turn north. Had he gone straight ahead, the Israelis would now own most of the oil in the Middle East. That may or may not have been good for them.

There are some lessons for us to learn from his experience and the keys decisions he made. We can equate them to your life. I am not a Christian, but as a professional spectator of Christianity, I can make these observations.

You have led many people out of the bondage of their sunday-school theology and have shown them a more powerful spirituality, one gained when pilgrims walk with Jesus of Nazareth. When you led them to a new place, you drowned the wrath of the fundamentalists who harassed them. Then you were like Moses when he reached the turning point of his journey. His fate was almost like the toss of a coin. You tossed the coin of life and got cancer, while others did not. Like Moses, you faced the consequences of the situation you are in and made a brave decision, which has made you a prophet to many about the mysteries of death.

In parting my friend, I say just this. You and I are brothers in a journey of faith that took us on different paths, but we have reached across those paths in mutual respect to the extent that I can say, MY BROTHER, I LOVE YOU.'

'A love that I return.'

They parted in silence.

———

Barton Deakin looked Graeme squarely in the eye. He saw strength, and he saw mateship.

'Before we work out how we should say farewell, could I just warn you that I have upset your friend, Donald Goldwater? I have given him a vivid description of my dark views of him and of his media interview with you. He was not at all pleased. He actually threatened to knock my block off, but then thought better of it. I extracted a sort of commitment that he would apologise to you to your face today and then again on his next show. Don't hold your breath, but there is a slight possibility it could happen.'

Graeme smiled while patting Barton on the shoulder and telling him that he was a good lad. They reminisced for a few short minutes about happy days they had enjoyed together, then shared a warm goodbye. Their relationship was one that they both cherished. It had embraced many memorable discussions about the great issues of the day, and they had supported one another in public debates on controversial issues.

A high five and a warm smile. Words seemed superfluous.

———

Aisha and Dalai were not quite the last to leave. Aisha held him close for a long time.

'You are a prophet whom the prophet Muhammad would be pleased to accept as an honoured partner. Your death will cause many to look death squarely in the eye and have no fear. You have reformed their end-of-life experience. I will see you tomorrow. It will be an unforgettable part of my life. You will always be my spiritual partner.'

'And for me too. No words I can say will be adequate at this moment.'

She departed before the tears could flow. Graeme watched her in admiration of a wonderful soul.

Dalai said his simple farewell. 'You have such infinite wisdom that, if you were a Confucian, you would be regarded as a supreme soul. In my mind, you will die with the fundamentals of Confucius as a partner of your magnificent Christian faith.'

'I will be proud to have the mind of Confucius as I die. Without detracting from your sincere comment, may I comment that Sarah, the Buddhist who was here tonight, declared that she believed I had acquired a Buddhist state of enlightenment?'

'This is delightful. I agree with Sarah. It proves that in the realm of faith and belief there are powerful connections between us.'

'We can agree on that, Dalai. As we say goodbye, I hope that you and Aisha will have a lifelong friendship.'

'We will. Our partnership has risen above the physical. It is beautifully spiritual. I cannot describe what it means to me, and I know that Aisha is of the same mind. Her presence enhances my life every day.'

'May it grow and grow and grow more beautiful every day.'

———

The very last was The Donald. 'I deliberately got myself into a spot where I could be sure of being the absolute last at the backend of the queue. I wanted to have a private word with you and, if I may suggest it, your wife and family too.'

Graeme signalled to Penelope, Luke and Fiona that they were welcome to come over to join in. Donald had already had a pleasant interlude with them as he worked the room during drinks. He could be a charmer when he was not broadcasting.

'Firstly, thank you all for inviting me to be here this evening. I did not deserve to be invited after the way I treated Graeme on my program.'

Penelope responded, 'I feel compelled to say that I was unhappy when Graeme said he was inviting you to be here, but he has always been a very forgiving person, so his action did not surprise me. Despite these reservations, we are happy you came.'

Donald then mentioned his spat with Barton and indicated that he had taken note of it.

'You are gracious,' he went on. 'I misjudged you, Graeme. I took the view that you were grandstanding so the publicity would create a new demand for your books and enhance your family's financial position for the long term. I found out later that you had not made any public statements before or after our public encounter. Others have done all the talking.

I also thought that you were using VAD to embarrass your Church as a final revenge for you to enjoy after your many disagreements with them. Your bishop has just cleared the air about this in my talk with him tonight. He is at a point in his thinking where he regards you as a modern prophet whose legacy should not be forgotten.

Thirdly, I had generated a dislike of you. As a non-Christian, I thought your books were just sensationalism. Frankly, I did not spend a moment trying to understand them. I now plan to read them. When our broadcast was over, I did a reassessment of my thinking because you handled yourself well. Then tonight I did have interesting conversations, not only with the bishop, but also with the rabbi, Pauline Palmer and Dalai, the Confucian guy. They all gave me some interesting insights that have broadened my mind on a few important issues relating to life and death. Then the legal guy put it all into starker focus.

Now, let me be clear. I am not about to have a Damascus Road conversion like St Paul. Nowhere remotely near it. May I add that I will always value my ratings as a broadcaster far more than any gentlemanly calling that may require me to admit my mistakes, or make apologies, or seek forgiveness—no matter how dark my sins.

But I do want to say this. You are a better person than I will ever be, and I have learned much from my experience of meeting you. I know now that while I had no control whatsoever over the circumstances of my birth, there is a real possibility that I could one day have a choice about the way I may die, and that is a choice that no one has the right to deny me, nor you.

I have learned and accepted that voluntary assisted dying is all about exercising our right as citizens to have freedom of choice. You have made that choice. Few will ever follow you in taking up that particular freedom of choice. As your legal friend forecasted, I may be too frightened to make it. But none of us must ever be told that we have no right to exercise it.'

'We appreciate your frankness,' said Fiona, and Luke endorsed her comment. Penelope gave him a friendly peck on the cheek, and Graeme shook his hand. The Donald then began to walk towards his car, but stopped for a final word or two.

'I think that Pauline is on to a great innovation with her not-for-profit companies. It has potential. But she is a very difficult person to understand, and her public-relations skills are somewhat deficient. She has trouble treating anyone else as an equal. I told her so quite bluntly, and that stunned her a bit, but I suggested to her that she make a serious effort to improve her relationships or she will be dead in the water. Asked the bishop to knock a bit of sense into her. Hope he does. Now, let me get to a much more important comment. I will stop in my tracks at 3pm tomorrow and wish your spirit an important journey into the hearts and minds of the more cynical, like me.'

———

Penelope and their children were in a state of mind that could only be described as spellbound. They were filled with unfathomable pride and joy that drowned all sense of sorrow and sadness.

Graeme drew them to him, and they hugged in what looked like a very formidable rugby scrum. When they let go, all four were smiling. Then he perpetuated the happy moment by enthusiastically inviting them to pour him a solid wee dram of one of his most revered single malt scotch whiskies.

It was from an old distillery situated on the Bonnie Bonnie banks of Loch Lomond, the most romantic of lakes in the world where, according to the great Scottish ballad, 'me and my true love were ever want to gae'.

He sipped it slowly and enjoyed every dram of it.

Penelope, Fiona and Luke sat there and watched with peace in their souls. No words were spoken nor needed. The silence was golden.

Chapter Twenty-One

It was scheduled to be the final day in the life of Graeme Brown, a good person who had lived for sixty quality years. He planned that it would be the happiest day of his eventful life.

For this one man, the mystery of eternity was just a few hours away from being solved. Graeme's life would end in a hospital at 3pm precisely. But at 9am, a roadblock occurred.

The situation could best be described by the words of Charles Dickens in the opening line of his famous novel *A Tale of Two Cities*: 'It was the best of times, it was the worst of times.'

The registrar of the Supreme Court called the Brown home at 9am. Luke took the call, and his face went pale white.

The Board of Disciples of the Pentecostal Church, at which Scott Palmer had been a member and Pauline was still a member, had a few moments ago filed an urgent injunction with the court to halt the death of Graeme Brown via voluntary assisted dying, scheduled for 3pm that very day. Justice Maureen O'Grady would hear the matter at 10am. She requested of Luke that he give notice of who would represent Graeme so that the relevant papers could be despatched.

Without hesitation, Luke declared that Barton Deakin would represent Graeme. The registrar stated that he knew the Dean of the Law School personally and indicated that he would contact him immediately. He actually sounded pleased to hear that Barton would appear for Graeme.

Luke looked at the invitation list for last night's party, which was lying on Graeme's desk. He found Barton's contact number and called him. The great man was shocked by this vile action and instantly declared that he would cancel his schedule for the day and be at the court at 10am without fail.

'Do not tell your father, mother or sister that this is happening. Leave it in my hands. I will fix it. This will be the performance of my legal career.'

Luke was worried about the judge presiding at the injunction hearing. 'Isn't Justice O'Grady a strict Roman Catholic who, in her private life, is a staunch opponent of VAD? She will almost certainly grant the injunction.'

'Your description of her is correct. Even so, her conservative outlook drives her to interpret laws strictly on what the wording of a law says. She won't play games with me. We know and respect one another. You and your family continue your day as planned. I will be in touch with you immediately after the hearing is completed and the judge announces her decision. Just stay totally firm that only you and I know that this is happening. I am impressed that you called me as soon as the court contacted you. You have acted wisely.'

The call ended. Luke was sick at heart, but he felt certain that the only person in the world who could fix this challenge was Barton Deakin.

The great lawyer was at that moment accepting that this challenge had been bound to happen. The local Pentecostal Church, having blotted their copybook in a significant way over Covid-19, was making an attempt to prove to the world that they stood for the sanctity of life. This gave them a chance to look like responsible people.

He was filled with disgust.

Barton walked into the elegant waiting room outside the personal chambers of Justice Maureen O'Grady at the Supreme Court. The furnishings and paintings inside were magnificently conservative.

Seated in the room was Judas Pontius, a high-profile barrister who had an infamous record for taking on any client for any cause so long as they paid him a massive fee in advance. He could not care less whether his clients won or lost. All he had to do was win enough cases so future clients would not hesitate to sign him up and pay big time.

Barton was certain that a significant portion of Pentecostal Church funds was already in the Pontius bank account. Judas appeared to be shocked that Barton had arrived. He had felt certain that Graeme Brown would not have had enough time to enlist someone of Barton's stature.

Barton greeted him with cold derision. 'At it again, eh, Pontius? Stealing money from churches this time. Is there any institution safe from your plundering tentacles?'

'You know how it is, Barton. The Church is very upset about VAD. It is entirely at odds with their beliefs, so they decided to make an example of the illegality of this particular case as a first step in getting VAD laws repealed.'

'Why didn't they do it last year when the laws went through parliament? Were they not upset then?'

'They wanted to last year, but did not know how to go about it. Scott Palmer retained me to give them guidance some months back. I advised them to wait for a high-profile VAD candidate, and then I would hit it hard. It is obvious that they will never again get a case more high profile than this one involving Graeme Brown.'

'I see Maureen's associate approaching us, so let's go inside and finish this nonsense quickly so you can crawl back into the gutter you have been living in for far too many long years.'

Judas had enough sense not to reply.

Justice Maureen O'Grady welcomed Barton warmly and Judas with cool courtesy. She invited them both to sit. Then she asked Judas to state, for her benefit and Barton's, the case supporting his application for an injunction to stop the death of Graeme Brown.

Judas was superb. He put in a big effort to earn his money. In essence, his case came down to two crucial issues. Firstly, the Pentecostal Church believed that voluntary assisted dying was suicide, pure and simple. The name was spin designed to make it sound decent and respectable. It was vital to the needs of a stable society that this matter be settled once and for all. Graeme Brown was planning for his suicide to happen today.

Judas continued, saying the Church believed that VAD was in defiance of one of the Ten Commandments, which says with clarity, 'THOU SHALT NOT KILL'. Genuine Christians cannot deviate from this. They are compelled to stop it. Not to do so would be an offence to God, as only God can determine who lives and who dies. The Church also believed that Graeme Brown was mentally unstable and therefore unfit to responsibly make the decision that he should die. One had only to read any of his seven books to determine that he was obsessed with denigrating churches, and that he went to extremes to do so. He was clearly an unbalanced person.

Judas then read several paragraphs from three of Graeme's books to prove his point. They were well chosen, as the words depicted three quite unstable people who behaved with outrageous irresponsibly. Judas demanded that the injunction be granted this very morning, right now. This would immediately halt plans for Graeme to die today. Once this was granted, the Church would honour an undertaking to bring a full case before the court as a matter of urgency.

Justice O'Grady did not ask any questions of clarification. She invited Barton to respond.

Barton pointed out in blunt and powerful terms that the legislation that was passed by parliament went to great lengths in detail clauses to emphatically distinguish between VAD and suicide, as it was expected this issue would one day be the subject of litigation. The wording ensured that it could never be successfully challenged in any court.

As Barton explained, if Her Honour felt that leave should be granted to hear such a case, it would take a minimum of two years to work its way through the legal system. So what is the point of denying Graeme the choice of using this legitimate legislation? It is the law, and he is entitled to use it.

Barton then took a huge risk that had the potential to offend Her Honour, devoted Catholic that she was, though he decided that it was a risk he had to take. He declared himself to be certain that the prolonged court hearings of such a case would eventually determine that any suicide of any type represented the sole right of a person to choose whether they wanted to take their own life at any time. It was their life, no one else was impacted by it. The whole concept of illegal suicide had been introduced to the world by judgemental religions, not by law makers. Christians, Muslims and anyone else must leave it to God to make the judgement on the matter. It was not their business.

Barton then took aim at the commandment 'THOU SHALT NOT KILL', pointing out to Her Honour that the words clearly refer to killing another person, not yourself. Some Bible translators even describe it as 'THOU SHALT NOT MURDER'. So we are discussing two different subjects. A person with a terminal illness who goes into a garage, turns on the car ignition and stays there until they die is not committing a murder.

'The learned counsel who represents the Church here today has emphatically declared that only God can decide who lives and dies. May I then pose this question? Why would a God who caused millions of Jews and Gypsies to die in the Holocaust be even slightly concerned about one man who chose to die in accordance with the laws of the land in which he lived?'

In addition, Barton pointed out to Her Honour that to declare Graeme Brown mentally unable to make a decision about VAD is a gross insult to a great man, especially coming from a Church that has acted with total insanity when it deliberately created conditions where many of its members, including Scott Palmer, died from Covid-19.

Barton spoke with controlled fury, 'It is an insult to God for them to falsely sit in judgement of anyone.'

Calming down, he asked Justice O'Grady if he could tell a story, one he did not seek to have admitted as evidence but which described the problems that churches, down the centuries, have had with people who did not fit in with their established traditions.

She agreed, so Barton began telling the story of Joseph Mohr, a priest who lived in Austria in the nineteenth century. In 1818, he composed a new Christmas carol to sing as a refreshing change from the usual ones. It was called 'Silent Night; Holy Night' and he sang it to his congregation on Christmas Eve. They were outraged that he had broken with their traditions and demanded that the bishop remove him from his role as parish priest. The bishop was even more outraged and sent Mohr to be priest in a poor village in a lonely part of Austria.

Mohr's family appealed to the King of Austria. To their delight, the King thought the new carol was magnificent and decreed that it must be sung in every church in Austria every Christmas for evermore. Now it is a worldwide favourite. A century later, when Bing Crosby sang it in America, it sold more recordings than any other carol in American history.

'My point is, Your Honour, that Graeme Brown is no more a wild heretic than Joseph Mohr. Brown's books are now read in all the nations where Mohr's carol is sung. To declare him to be mentally ill would be a grave injustice. May I add, Your Honour, that last night, I was privileged to attend a function that Graeme Brown held at his home to say farewell, face to face, to fifty of his closest friends. He made a speech, and I recorded it. With your permission, I will play it so you can determine whether, less than a day ago, this man was mentally unstable.'

Her Honour agreed, and Barton played the recording.

She was clearly moved but maintained her conservative demeanour. Looking at Judas, she emphatically stated that the speech was not given by a man with mental problems rendering him unable to distinguish between whether he wanted to live or die.

Judas did not give in. He fought on. His clients had to get a run for their money.

'No evidence has been provided that it is Brown that we just listened to,' said Judas.

Barton then mentioned to Her Honour that a member of the Pentecostal Church which is bringing this case before the court, was present at the function. Her name was Pauline Palmer and he had her phone number.

'With your permission,' said Barton, 'I will call her, and I respectfully suggest that you should speak with her, not me. She must be made aware that she is giving evidence before a court.'

Pauline came on the line. Justice Maureen O'Grady introduced herself, asked sufficient questions to identify herself, then carefully explained all facets of the legal situation that she was about to determine. She invited Pauline Palmer to comment.

'Your Honour,' said Pauline, 'I have met Graeme Brown four times. We are not friends, but we have a professional relationship. I do not support his decision to die by VAD, either on moral or theological grounds. However, I have not the slightest doubt that he is in full possession of his mental faculties and clearly understands the finality of the step he will take today to end his life. My Church has every right to disagree with his proposed action, but it did not consult me on this matter and has no right to stop him from doing what is lawful and clearly his personal will.'

Justice O'Grady ended the call after thanking Pauline and receiving her confirmation that Graeme did make the speech she had just listened to. Without hesitation, she then addressed the two legal counsel who sat before her.

'The plea for an injunction is denied. Graeme Brown's planned death today is lawful and will proceed. He is clearly able to make the decision to use a law operable at this moment. Thank you and good morning.'

She signalled the end of the meeting. Both men stood, thanked her and left.

Outside, Barton said to Judas, 'Tell your Christian client that they collectively belong with you in your miserable little gutter, a long way from the paths that Jesus of Nazareth trod. However, I give thanks that there are many fine Churches in the world that operate with much higher standards of human behaviour.'

Barton walked away, calling Luke when he was out of earshot.

'It is all systems go, Luke. I will brief you on the details after Graeme has passed on. All that you need to know is that Justice Maureen O'Grady acted as a solid Christian will always act. Her Roman Catholic upbringing was on full display. She knows that truth and responsibility in Christianity are indivisible.'

Chapter Twenty-Two

little earlier, Graeme and his family had enjoyed a pleasant breakfast debating in a very positive manner what was the most significant event in Graeme's personal life, and what event in the history of the world in Graeme's era had the greatest impact on humanity.

He made it clear what they already knew. The greatest moments of life were the day that he first caught sight of Penelope while preaching a sermon at church, and when he caught his first glimpse of Luke and Fiona at their birth. Beyond that was the day when he learned he would die of cancer and gratefully found that it caused him no fear of death. Indeed, he welcomed it as an experience that was inevitable, but which had just come a little sooner than he expected.

The greatest historical event in Graeme's era caused much animated debate, but it was clear to them that it was climate change as the most likely event to destroy humanity in the long term.

Then Graeme left home for the last time. As he got into Penelope's car, he took one final look at the place that he had spent so many happy years. The memories flooded in. It was a beautiful home in which he shared his life with three beautiful people. No man could have been more blessed.

Penelope drove them down to the place in the park where Graeme had sat under a fine old tree to ponder his life and death just three months ago, minutes after Aisha had conveyed to him his fate. It was a physical struggle for Graeme as they strolled for a kilometre along the riverbank enjoying the sunshine and fresh air. There was no way that he would reveal to them any pain. Anyway, his walking stick gave him something to lean on.

Then Penelope drove them out of the city to the national park, the same one where Graeme's ashes would live on in the life of a beautiful young tree. If there were any juices in his ashes, he hoped they would sink into the soil and be part of this fine forest.

Not far from the very spot where the tree would grow, they found a little café that had been operated for many years by the trustees of the park. It was set in a newly planted rainforest near a small waterfall that represented the water of life.

Penelope had arranged for a private table to be set up for them on a flat rock almost under the falls. It really was a romantic place and its founders created it as an act of love. A wealthy family had donated the funds. They had lost a daughter who was struck down by a rare disease. She was a lover of trees. They made sure that her love of trees would be survived by the people gathering in this place.

Graeme enjoyed his favourite meal—German sausages with gravy and mashed potato, washed down with a superb glass of pinot noir. Fiona remarked that the sausages were not good for his diet. Graeme promised, under solemn oath, that he would never eat them again.

'While we are on this subject of my personal needs,' said Graeme, 'I must say that among my emails this morning was one from my tailor who sent it to all his clients. He has some top-quality shirts handmade in Milan. Says they will make me look like the trendiest guy in the world. I thought about the offer for a while but finally decided I did not really need them.'

They chatted about which was the most entrancing site each one had seen in their travels. Luke declared that it was the Sistine Chapel at the Vatican. Graeme asked him why.

'Well, Graeme, it is firstly a magnificent piece of art painted with extraordinary dedication and skill by Michelangelo, working for years as he lay painfully on his back on a suspended plank. I have often wondered what the basis was of his dedicated focus. Was it his love or fear of God, or just his incredible commitment to art as a powerful means of spreading the faith to millions of people beyond the Church? I actually think that he tried to achieve eternal life through his paintings. He did, except that it was in a different form to his expectation. His incredible work is still viewed a thousand years later by people from all over the world every year. I have a feeling that the modern Church is not seriously using art as a means of convincing people that the Christian life is a great one and that they should experience the beauty of it.'

Fiona was next. 'It is the Taj Mahal,' she said. 'An unforgettable highlight of my life has been that wonderful, around-the-world family holiday you took us on that included a fascinating time in India. As you know, we found the building to be magnificently beautiful. And on the day that we were there, large dark storm clouds provided an incredible background. The story of its creation taught me a lot about life. A very wealthy man of royal blood had been grossly unfaithful to his wife. When she died, he tried to convince the world of his great love for her by building this lovely place in her honour. Most people have now woken up to the fact that he was a fraud.

It raises the question of how many lovers have superficial partnerships. I am wondering, Graeme, how many of your numerous critics will now fall in love with you, go public with their conversion experience, and then write opinion pieces claiming that they have always been your closest admirer?'

'Too many,' said Graeme. 'Happily, I won't be around to read them, and I hereby issue an edict forbidding you to read a single one of them.'

Then Penelope had her say. 'When Graeme and I married,' she said, 'we were, compared to our modern comfortable lifestyle, as poor as church mice. We had no surplus money to go anywhere exciting for our honeymoon.

But a miracle occurred. An old bachelor, who had attended our church all his life, took us aside on the Sunday before our wedding and told us that he owned a small cottage in the mountains about an hour's drive away. He would be very honoured if we would accept his offer to stay there for a week free of charge. He would drive us there, then come back to pick us up a week later. He would stock the cottage with food and drinks as his wedding gift to us and would ensure it was spotless before we got there.

We gratefully accepted his offer, and we had a wonderful week. We climbed every mountain, forded every stream, followed every rainbow, swam every lake and talked with all the wildlife, not seeing another human for the entire week. It has been unforgettable. Far more wonderful than our stay in the Somerset Maugham suite at Raffles Hotel in Singapore years later. In that week of absolute peace and solitude, Graeme and I really got to know and understand one another. We can honestly say that, except for a few too many silly little domestic spats down the years, we have never lost the closeness we achieved at that little cottage.'

'I can but say Amen,' was Graeme's swift response as he began his own memory. 'After I had struck success as an author, Penelope and I did a lot of travelling to research my future books. I decided that one would be based in Tibet. By that time, I had met the Dalai Lama on a few occasions, and I called him to discuss my thoughts about my next book. Even though he was then living in refuge in India, he arranged for us to stay in a remote monastery in Tibet where the monks would educate us about the history of their ancient land and would teach us the art of meditation. We stayed there for several days. The accommodation was spartan but very clean, and life was well organised. The view of the Himalayas was incredible, and the silence was deafening. When the time came for us to leave, Penelope and I had a new vision of life. And as an author, I learned from those monks that a volume of words has little relevance. It is the choice of words that really matters. This means that the few words we speak at 3pm today will be our lasting memory.'

They sat silently as they pondered this. It enhanced the happiness of their day.

Without going home, they drove slowly to St Mark's Hospital, owned and managed by the Anglican Church. They chatted enthusiastically about the scenic landmarks that Graeme was seeing for the last time.

Aisha met them in the foyer and escorted them to a private room especially set up to carry out the procedure of voluntary assisted dying. It was not used often, but its usage was increasing. Today, it looked like a picture, with delightful arrangements of flowers placed around the room and the windows opened to let in the sunlight.

With a nurse assisting Aisha, and Graeme's family lawyer and a police officer present as witnesses, Graeme was prepared to take the action that only he could finally implement. He alone could press the button that released the lethal injection that would kill him without pain in seconds.

The policewoman stepped forward to ask Graeme one final time whether or not he wished to proceed. In a clear strong voice, he gave a response of yes. Both she and the lawyer signed a document that legally and finally recorded Graeme's answer. He countersigned it with a clear firm hand.

Penelope, Fiona and Luke gave him a warm embrace and then laid their hands upon him gently and tenderly. As prearranged, the music system played 'Ol' Man River', Graeme's favourite song, sung as an African American spiritual by a great human rights patriot, Paul Robeson, who was one of the inspirational heroes of his life. He silently sang along with it.

> He don't plant taters
> He don't plant cotton
> An' them that plants 'em is soon forgotten
> But ol' man river,
> He just keeps rollin' along

Then as friends from many nations around the world at that very moment stood in respectful silence, even though for some it was in the middle of the night, Graeme took the action that he had often debated and that was now clearly and indelibly embedded in his mind.

His reached out his hand, firmly and deliberately, to press the deadly button as he looked with unbounded love one last time at his cherished family, and they responded with love that knew no boundaries.

Across the edge of eternity, without a single tear being shed, their eyes met and held.

Courage on 9/11

On 11 September, 2001, Osama bin Laden masterminded the destruction of the World Trade Centre Towers in New York.

Of the many thousands who died, there were 200 who fell in trying to escape or jumped from the Towers to avoid being burned to death.

The media put special focus on a man and a woman who made a decision that it was preferable to die by being smashed against concrete than by burning to death. They had no other choice.

They held hands all the way down.

Their insurance policies, and other matters relating to their estates, would be determined on whether or not their deaths were acts of suicide.

The matter reached the courts where a judge declared that they had not committed suicide.

They had simply brought forward the time of their inevitable death.

Graeme Brown has just made exactly the same decision.

End Notes

Every one of us has the potential to be a storyteller, but few of us get around to telling our stories or relating a story about others. I have been threatening to tell this story at various times during the four decades that have passed since I first began my advocacy of voluntary euthanasia, now better known as voluntary assisted dying.

It was hard to find many supporters back in those earlier days, but positive public opinion began to grow steadily, and I eventually became a life member of a splendid community institution called Dying with Dignity, wonderful people who have toiled ceaselessly to have VAD legalised in Australia.

This meant that I could work with a team of great people, such as Jos Hall, Jeanette Wiley and Sid Finnigan. We were soon joined by influential VAD advocates David Muir, Peter Johnstone and Lindsay Marshall of the Clem Jones Foundation, and Andrew Denton and Kiki Paul of Go Gentle.

This endeavour has led me to write *A Beautiful Sunset* because I believe that if voluntary assisted dying can be seen by the community as a honourable human action more people will accept it as a right they can exercise if they wish to do so.

Of course, no book of quality can ever be written without the help of others, and I proudly acknowledge the fine work done by special friends of mine in helping me to bring *A Beautiful Sunset* to fruition:

Greg Cary, radio talkback host of legend and a long-time friend.

George Browning, retired Anglican bishop, with whom I have shared a spiritual journey of many decades.

Merrilyn and Wayne Hooper, valued friends for more than half a century in our active lives in church and society.

Suzie Ma, my local doctor, who does a wonderful job of keeping me alive.

Dr Karen Stenner, a long time adviser and friend who is one of the world's eminent political scientists.

John Harrison, who lectures in journalism at the University of Queensland. He was also my mentor in helping me publish my most recent books, *The Man on the Twenty Dollar Notes* and *Dinner with the Founding Fathers*.

I would like to especially thank my wife of sixty-two years, Helen, who has a loving ability to tell me frankly when the things that I say are sometimes right and often wrong.

None of these friends are responsible in any way for what I have said in *A Beautiful Sunset*. All of its defects are totally mine. The good things reflect their thoughts.

May I say also what a privilege it has been to work with Marcus Fielding and Duncan Strachan at Echo Books? They are a professional and helpful team of creative book publishers.

Writing *A Beautiful Sunset* has not been all that difficult, because I passionately believe in our right to choose to die with dignity. I have expressed what is deep in my soul. A background to the thoughts that I have expressed in this novel has been the historical fact that I have been at church for most Sundays of my eighty-nine years, during which my sixty-two years as an elder of the Presbyterian and Uniting Churches have enabled me to share quality time with many people at the time of their death.

Most handled well their end-of-life experience. Some reacted badly. The former is infinitely better.

Grace and peace,

Everald

About the Author

Everald Compton is an Australian who is approaching the tenth decade of his life.

Born and bred in rural Queensland, he studied accountancy and marketing while working in a bank and in an accountant's practice.

He then became an international fund-raising consultant working on community projects in 26 nations.

In his 'retirement' years, he became a company director, most notably as a Founding Director of National Seniors Australia and as the Founder of Australia's Inland Railway.

He also launched a successful career as an author, writing *The Man on the Twenty Dollar Notes* based on the life of Flynn of the Inland who founded the Royal Flying Doctor Service, and *Dinner with the Founding Fathers*, the story of the creation of the Australian nation in 1901.

However, he believes that *A Beautiful Sunset* is his finest literary achievement.

He has been a committed Christian since his Sunday School days out in the bush and has served as an Elder of the Presbyterian and Uniting Churches for more than six decades.

Interfaith dialogue and cooperation is now an important part of his life as is his active role as Chair of ACTS, a Uniting Church charity that provides financial aid to people in need.

Importantly, he leads Christians for Dying with Dignity.

In 1993, he became a Member of the Order of Australia for services to the community and received the Centenary Medal in 2001 for service to the Transport Industry.

He is an Adjunct Professor at the University of Queensland serving as Chair of the Advisory Panel of CRC Longevity, and an Honorary Senior Fellow of the University of the Sunshine Coast serving in the Thompson Institute for Mind and Neuroscience.

He lives in Brisbane with his wife, Helen. Their four children and eight grandchildren live in Brisbane, Melbourne, New York and Wiltshire UK.